Hail Mary

PLAYING FOR KEEPS
BOOK FOUR

SAMANTHA BARRETT

This is your warning!

If domestic violence, bullying, drug use, stalking, date rape,
loss of a loved one and degrading is a trigger for you then
close the book and move on to another amazing read.
If you are into some dark shit and get off on possessive as
fuck asshole alpha males, turn the page babe and wrap your
heart in a condom because these boys are about to fuck your
feelings, real hard!

For Sarah,
Dear lord woman, you keep me fucking humble and ride my ass like no other! Karma… I mean Alexa reminds me so much of you, this was always meant to be your book. Thank you from the bottom of my heart for always loving, caring, and being by my side throughout this journey. I fucking love you, lady!
Hail Mary sure as fuck is for you! Xxx

PROLOGUE

Alexa

"No more, Alexa. Jason is a dick and I won't stand by and watch him hurt you any longer, he is a piece of shit!" I lean my head against the car window and gaze out at the passing landscape trying to tune out Cody's bitching, I know she's right. Jason is a dick, since we started dating six months ago he has changed. When he became captain of the basketball team at our high school it went to his head, three months ago he started hitting me and no matter how hard I try to end things, he won't let me. "Do you hear me?"

I cringe and slowly turn to look at my sister, who is gripping the steering wheel so tight her knuckles are white. "Uh, yeah." She pulls her gaze from the road to glare at me for a second and I quickly look away.

"I mean it, Lexi. Jason is a piece of shit and after everything my friend Leah went through–."

That piques my interest. "What happened? Did she get beaten up by her boyfriend and call her sister to come to save her ass?"

Cody huffs and shakes her head, clearly she's exasperated by me. "Not exactly, a guy did punch her though after airing a video of him raping her at a party, he roofied her drink then aired it at a football game. She's in Alaska at the moment trying to recover and heal."

"Her brother is the one you have been hooking up with, right?" Cody cringes but nods. "You lecture me on my choices, yet you're sleeping with a guy who won't commit to you."

"We're not talking about me, Lexi. Corvin isn't going to beat me to death. He may not want to commit but at least he keeps his hands to himself."

I snicker. "Whatever, can we just not talk about this shit?"

"If Jason kills you, I have first dibs on your Gucci bag and clothes."

My jaw slackens as I turn to scowl at the bitch. "Seriously?" She just giggles and shrugs her shoulders. "Well, if your boy toy kills you, I'll be a good sister and fuck him over so bad he'll hate himself and wish he was the one who had died."

"Jesus, Lexi, that is fucking morbid."

I scoff. "Coming from the one who just wants my shit when my ex kills me."

"Alexa, if Jason ever took you from me, I would ruin his life and kill the son of bitch with my bare hands. We may fight and joke but at the end of the day, you're my baby sister and there isn't a fucking thing in this world I wouldn't do to keep you safe."

I wish I had known then that this conversation would in fact become my reality. Revenge is a dish best served hot, ready or not, Corvin Williams, I'm coming in blazing.

CHAPTER ONE

"I can't do this," I breathe out the moment the priest begins to speak, it's too fucking much for me to handle.

"You may not want to be here but by God, you are going to stay because that girl deserves that much from you. Man the hell up, Corvin, and pull your head out of your ass. Cody deserves more than this pathetic sack of shit in front of me. Don't dishonor her by being a pussy and leaving." I stare at Darius, surprised by the amount of contempt I hear in his voice. He has no idea that it is taking every ounce of strength I have just to stand here, that wooden box that holds her body taunts me.

"Who the fuck is she?" Beck growls from the other side of Darius.

"Who?" D asks.

"Her!" Beck grits out as he points toward the front of the church where–fuck! It's the girl from the motel this morning. I was that fucking wasted last night I don't even remember who the fuck she is. Honestly, if we fucked I'd be surprised my cock even got hard with the state I was in if the hangover I'm currently dealing with is anything to go by.

"Shit," Darius breathes out at the sight of her. The girl lifts her gaze and locks eyes with me. A chill runs down my spine, I can feel it in the pit of my stomach that she wasn't just some random groupie from around here that has watched me play.

"Thank you all for coming," she says as she looks around the packed church. "For those of you who don't know me, my name is Alexa." She turns her gaze back to me. I swallow the dread brewing inside me, I know without a doubt that she is about to tip my fucking world upside down. "And I'm Cody's little sister."

Jesus Christ!

I feel sick. Her mouth continues to move but I can't hear anything over the ringing in my ears, it becomes hard to pull air into my lungs. My head starts to spin and my stomach churns. I shove past Darius and Beckett and rush outside, jump down the stairs and manage to make it around the corner of the church before I empty the contents of my stomach in the garden. Fuck. Beer coming back out of your body like this tastes like fucking ass.

"Fucking hell, look at the state of you," Beck growls from behind me. I ignore the bastard. I don't need any of their judgment, they're no fucking saints. The thing is at least they get to still see the women they love unlike me, I have to bury the girl who gave me everything only for me to refuse her and treat her like shit.

"Well, what a surprise." At the sound of her voice, I straighten and wipe my mouth with the back of my hand before I slowly turn around and face Cody's little sister. Her long raven-colored hair falls in loose waves around her shoulders, bright blue eyes spear me with a look of hatred. She's so tiny, the top of her head would just reach my chest. Looking at her is like looking at a pocket-sized version of Cody. Pain radiates throughout my chest.

"We just came to pay our respects–" Beck starts but she isn't listening, her gaze is fixated on me as she talks over him.

"The fact you have the nerve to show your face here

speaks volumes about you being a real piece of shit." I flinch but don't deny what she says, because it's true. I shouldn't be here.

"Hey, Cody and Corv were—" She swings her gaze to Darius and pins him a scathing look before cutting off his tirade.

"I don't give a fuck what any of you have to say." She slowly turns back to me but this time, her face is blank of all emotions. "Because of you, I have to bury my sister on her nineteenth birthday." The air rushes from my lungs, I had no fucking idea today was her birthday. "You may not know this yet, Corvin, but in time you will learn that Cody was the nice sister, the one who loved everyone and saw the world through rose-colored glasses." I frown. "I'm the opposite. I'm jaded and fucking angry, I hate everyone and live to ruin those who wrong me or anyone I care about. You just became my sole focus. Everywhere you look, everywhere you go I'll be watching and waiting for you to fuck up. The moment you do, I'll be the one calling the cops and sending your ass to jail because, make no mistake, my sister and I shared *everything* with each other." She doesn't wait for a reply, turns on her heel and marches her little ass back inside the church.

"Why do I get a sinking feeling that she is going to cause us a shit load of problems?' Darius breathes out.

"Because I think Alexa Sutton just admitted to the fact that her sister told her about me taking care of Garett," I answer. I feel their gazes on me, but mine is still glued to the little demon that just rocked me to my core and gave me the reality check I needed to get my shit together.

CHAPTER TWO

Corvin

Six weeks later

Have you ever felt a pain so crippling that it steals the very breath from your lungs and makes you feel like you're dying slowly, except you're not? You just have to force yourself to breathe through the pain and then carry on like you want to be here. You watch people smile and laugh and think to yourself, how the fuck can you be happy when she's dead?

She's in a wooden box buried in the dirt where sooner rather than later bugs are going to eat away at her decomposing body—all you have left is memories. That's the thing though, no one tells you when you lose someone you love that memories are the hardest fucking part. Every time you catch yourself daydreaming, it's about them. Or, when you lay in bed and try to sleep, it's their face you see every time you close your damn eyes. I thought moving away from CHU and leaving the team to train one on one with the best trainer in the country would help ease the pain because I'd have something else to focus on—it didn't.

Living away from the others has been a blessing. Beck's in Alaska with *her* and Dawson, Saint and Crue moved into the dorms on campus to be closer to Katie. Darius packed up and took Leah to Chicago, where she studies online and he learns the ropes of HQ. Me, I packed my shit and moved to North Carolina to train to be the best the fucking QB so I can get drafted. The penthouse I live in is luxurious. The place is huge and something any guy my age would fucking love but I hate it. Her laughter doesn't fill the place, her intoxicating perfume doesn't linger after she's left the room, and stray hairs don't stick my pillowcase.

I'm fucking drowning without her and I don't know how to fix it. I stopped drinking the day we buried her, haven't popped a single pill since then either. All I do is hit the gym, train, hit the gym again, then come home to work on the reports Darius and Beck send me. It was supposed to be just them doing this shit so Saint, Crue and I could focus on football but with too much free time on my hands, I needed something to occupy my mind since I don't have school anymore. Not going to school is going to fucking make it hard to get drafted but I can't go back there, everything reminds me of her.

Like clockwork my phone pings with a text like it does at eleven forty-two every day—the time Cody was officially pronounced dead.

ALEXA

> Did you know she wanted to star in Rita Ora's film clips one day as a backup dancer? No, of course, you wouldn't because all you ever fucking cared about was yourself. I hope to God her fucking death haunts you every second of every day, you piece of shit! I. Hate. You!

Scrubbing a hand down my face I release a loud exhale. Every day since the funeral, Alexa texts me something about Cody and then always ends the message with wishing me dead or hoping I'm in pain. Honestly, at the start, I hated them and felt like a right fucking cunt for how I treated Cody, but now, I love learning new things about her each day. It's sick and twisted but it's the only link I have to her.

> I didn't know that. She wouldn't have been a backup dancer, she was far too beautiful and would have stolen the spotlight.

Her reply comes almost instantly.

ALEXA

> Go fuck yourself, also your car needs another paint job!

"Fucking hell," I growl into the empty apartment. I don't know how she found out I moved, but two days after I moved into the penthouse, Alexa showed up with a bat in her hand where I train and smashed the windshield of my new Maserati. I should have let the cops arrest her but the guilt of knowing it's my fault that she is struggling and unable to live her life like she used to stopped me. She's keyed my car, smashed the mirrors, tried to break into the penthouse, and slandered me online—Katie was able to remove all of that shit. The girl lives to torment me and I'm unable, or unwilling to stop her.

> I'll sort it, is there a color you prefer or just get the red touched up for you to ruin again?

I shouldn't taunt her but Alexa is the only person who I want to speak to right now, I constantly blow off the others and only communicate through emails in regards to work. I know they are all worried about me and scared that I am going to throw any chance I have of being drafted, but the truth is, as much as I love the game and thrive off the need to be the best QB in the country, some of my focus has shifted from that goal and now I'm just stuck in a state of limbo wondering where the fuck I go from here. I know if I give that up, I will hate myself for it in a few years' time, but then another part wonders if all the stress and pressure is worth it.

ALEXA

Go fuck yourself pretty boy, I hope you break your arm!

Oh goodie, she must be warming up to me since she didn't tell me to go die this time!

Training with Travis is brutal. He pushes me harder than I have ever trained before. The guy doesn't push you to be an ass, he pushes because he can see the best in you and wants your full potential to be obtainable. My muscles ache in the best possible way. I used to detest ice baths but now they have become my saving grace. Travis is pushing me to sign up at the local college and join the team as their QB. The idea does intrigue me but I'm not ready to *people* every day. I lean my head back and close my eyes as I wait for the fifteen-minute timer to count down, letting me know to get my ass out of the ice bath and head home.

"You're good, Corvin." I blink one eye open and stare over at Travis.

"Thanks," I say closing my eyes again.

"That wasn't a compliment." I snap my eyes open and glare over at him. "You could be great but something is holding you back. I have a buddy over at Wake Forest College that is willing to put in a good word for you."

Shaking my head I answer him. "I'm not interested–"

"Too late, their QB is injured and I told them you would be there first thing Monday morning, so sort your shit over the weekend and get your ass there first thing." Before I can even argue or call him out for going behind my back, the asshole turns and leaves the fucking locker room, while I sit here stewing in my anger.

Fuck this!

I don't even wait for the timer, I get out and change before storming out to the parking lot ready to get the fuck out of here, until I can't spot my car. I turn a full circle looking for it. It's not fucking hard to miss, it's a cherry red Maserati for fuck's sake and I always park in the same spot–right in front of the doors! This can't be happening, there is no fucking way someone had the balls to steal my fucking car in broad daylight!

Unless...

I pull my phone out of my pocket and immediately see a string of messages from Alexa and just know without a doubt it was her who stole my fucking car! My finger hovers over the message thread for a second before I grow some fucking balls and click on it.

"Mother fucking, bitch licking, pussy hairy cunt!" I spew out and cringe the moment I hear a gasp but don't dare turn around. Alexa stole my fucking car alright and had the cahoonies to fucking send me pictures of the damage she has caused to it. The little bitch has taken a baseball bat to the headlights and bonnet of my beautiful MC20 Cielo Spyder, the cherry-red paint is ruined thanks to her keying the sides, all four tires have a knife sticking out of each of them. The last photo has a cold sweat breaking out on my brow. It's a picture of a Zippo lighter next to a jerrycan. Before I can even think, I hit dial on her contact and wait with bated breath for her to answer.

"How can I help you, your royal worthlessness?" I grit my teeth at the smug tone of her voice and remind myself to remain calm or risk the little psycho burning my baby to a crisp.

"That's a five hundred thousand dollar car that you are about to set fire to–"

"What do you mean *about to*?"

My stomach sinks. "You already burnt it, didn't you?"

"Yep." The way she pops that *'p'* like she is so fucking proud of herself grates on my fucking nerves. A slow smile spreads across my face when the sound of sirens can be heard in the background, her sharp intake of air tells me she is still at the scene of the crime.

"Well, now that you burnt your getaway car, how do you plan to evade the cops?"

"Fuck you, *dickbag!*" The line goes dead and for the first time in weeks laughter bursts out of me. I have no fucking idea why I'm hunched over laughing so fucking hard when my car is burnt out on the side of the road somewhere. But, knowing that Alexa is about to get busted and will receive a taste of her own medicine after all these weeks, has me puffing out my chest and smiling.

Standing at the counter in my kitchen I dig into my boiled chicken, asparagus and brown rice. I get my meals prepped and delivered every Sunday. I'm on a strict diet to stay in shape and I'll admit since getting back to training and cutting down on all the carbs, I am starting to feel like my old self again, physically. I finish up and toss the container in the trash before heading into the living room. The silence of this penthouse haunts me. I'm not used to living alone and I hate to fucking admit it, but I miss my brothers. I just don't know how to be around… them right now. I know shit is hard for all of us and everyone is dealing with the loss of… *her*. It's March and I have mere months to get my shit together if I want to get drafted. Saint and Crue have both been training their asses off and I know without a doubt they will both be scouted but the question is, what happens if they don't make the same team?

The shrill sound of my ringtone pierces the air and pulls me from my thoughts. I hit answer without checking the I.D.

"This is a collect call from the North Carolina police department from inmate–" The automated voice changes and I smirk at the sound of hers. "Alexa." I can hear the loathing in her tone and know it must be killing her to have had to call me. *"Will you accept the charges?"*

"Yes."

A second later her tone fills the silence. "I need you to bail me out." I roll my lips over my teeth to keep from laughing, I don't know what the hell it is about this girl but she is the only one who has been able to pull me from my sullen moods with her hateful messages. It's crazy but talking to her every day has become something I have come to rely on, crave even.

"Now, why on God's good green earth would I do that?"

A tiny growl fills the line and this time I can't help the laugh that erupts from me, it feels so strange to laugh again.

"Look, I have a court date set and they already told me they tracked you down and asked if you wanted to press charges."

"Is there a question in there?"

Again, she growls and I laugh at the frustration evident in her tone. "Can you bail me out or not? I know you didn't press charges or I would have been stuck here."

I pretend to mull over her question and then let out a dramatic sigh. "You see, I would love to but I don't have a car to come downtown because your crazy ass burnt it! Enjoy your night in the cells and a word of advice, my little vexed friend, don't drop the soap." I end the call and drop my phone on the sofa beside me smiling like a fool at the fact I finally got the upper hand over Alexa Sutton. Then guilt hits me, she's in that cell right now because of what I did to her sister. If I wasn't such a coward, that poor girl wouldn't even be there.

CHAPTER THREE

Alexa

I slam the phone back in the cradle and stomp my foot like a petulant child. That motherfucker! I had hoped that his guilt would win him over and he'd drag his happy ass down here and bail me out! I turn eighteen in September, so I'm technically still a minor and the fact I didn't have ID on me when the cops caught me running is the only reason my parents weren't called. I lied and told the woman that allowed me to use the phone that I was calling my boyfriend. I almost gag at the thought of Corvin ever being anything to me. It was either call him or Jason. Dumb as it sounds, it was easier to call him than let my fucking ex know where the hell I am. The guy is hunting my ass down since I flushed his stash. I didn't know at the time that all those pills weren't his and may have cost him a couple of grand, so he wants me for payback.

"Back to your cell." I groan and follow the woman back, no point bitching about it. I did the crime, now I guess I'll have to do the time.

Fuck my life.

When the metal bars clang shut behind me, I flinch. It smells like piss and dirty balls in here. It's not jail, so the cells here have both men and women in them. I've never been so grateful to be under eighteen in my life, my age is the only reason I'm in my own cell and not sharing with big Bertha beside me. That woman is double the size of my father and looks like she could crack my skull with her bare fucking hands! I lay down on the bench seat that is attached to the back wall and close my eyes. I have no one else to blame for my predicament but myself. I threw away my chance at CHU by following Corvin fucking Williams here to North Carolina. See, the thing is, I'm smart and was able to graduate early and start college. I scored a free-ride scholarship with housing and everything to CHU, but then that all changed, none of it meant anything when I lost my best friend, my sister.

I feel the first tear slide down the side of my face and scrunch my eyes tighter, trying to force them back. I hate this. I hate everything and everyone. I hate my parents for not blaming Corvin and allowing him to walk free, they didn't even press charges and urged me to drop this *insane concept* as they like to call it. I'm surprised they haven't reported me missing yet. Mind you, they probably have no idea I've even left the state. No matter how good my grades were or the number of awards I would get at school, they still wouldn't notice me. It was always about Cody and Keeley—our older sister who has graduated college and moved to Thailand with her fiancé. I was the kid that should never have won the race to my mother's egg, the unwanted child.

"Sutton, you're free to go." I swipe away the tears, sit up and look over at the guard confused as hell. The moment she opens the cell, I clamp my mouth closed and decide not to ask questions and just get the fuck out of here. The moment I'm handed back my things and told to stay out of trouble, I book it out of the precinct after agreeing to show up for my court date. Stepping outside I breathe in the nighttime air and sigh. It's cold out, so I tug my jacket closed at the front and descend the concrete stairs only to slam to a halt when I see a teal Maserati MC20 Cielo Spyder, the exact same model as the one I burnt out earlier today. The moment the driver's side opens, I know who it is already. The smug son of a bitch stands there with a smirk on his face.

"Jail bait, good to see you again." My nostrils flare and my body stiffens at the sight of the man I hate more than anything in this fucking cruel world.

"I would have rather walked in on my parents fucking than be seeing you again." The ghost of a smile drops from his face at the harsh tone of my voice, his eyes harden as he looks me over.

"Get in."

"I'd rather crawl across shards of glass than go anywhere with a murderer like you." My words hit their mark, his face morphs into a look of pain. Good, I want him to feel every ounce of pain I do.

"Get in the car, Alexa."

I scoff and shake my head as I take two steps forward, leaving an inch of space between me and the car as I stare directly into his eyes. "Go fuck yourself, Corvin," I spit and turn on my heel, I make it two steps before his words have me freezing.

"You'll be breaking your bail conditions."

I slowly turn to face him, the devilish glint in his eyes tells me I'm about to be blindsided. "What conditions?" I force each word out through clenched teeth.

He smiles smugly and winks–he fucking winks at me like we are old chums! "You needed an address to be bailed too and Troy, my lawyer gave them mine since we found out you don't have one and have been living in the abandoned house off Trolsone." My eyes widen a fraction. I look him over and admit to myself that I have clearly underestimated him, he isn't just some dumb rich jock.

"Fuck you very much, dickface, but I'll pass," I snarl as I attempt to leave again, but this time I don't even make it a step before his words force me to a stop yet again.

"All your shit is in the trunk. I cleared that shit hole of a house out. You walk away now, Alexa, and I walk my ass in that station and snitch you out. They'll lock your little ass up until your court date. Now, get the fuck in the car because my patience is running the fuck out."

The pair of us stand here glaring at each other, his eyes spark with fire the longer he stares at me, that dead look he's been sporting for weeks slowly fades and I fucking hate it! I want this son of a bitch to feel every ounce of pain I feel. I want him to suffer and feel like he is suffocating every day he wakes up like I am. He doesn't deserve to live. But, an idea strikes, if I have to stay with him that means I can fuck shit up for him from the inside.

I smile wide and act like a ditsy blonde twirling my hair around my index finger and bite my bottom lip. I fucking love how his face drops and he straightens at the sight. He knows I'm up to something and clearly, he is regretting ever allowing his address to be used now.

"Well, when you put it like that, stud, who am I to refuse you and your kind offer?" I make sure to put on the best southern drawl I can. He eyes me skeptically as I make my way over to the car, open the door and claim my seat. It takes him a couple of seconds before he folds his tall muscular body into the car. The moment he closes the door the car suddenly feels too small, his scent and sheer nearness over-whelm me. I shift until I'm plastered against the door getting as far away from the reaper as I can. He pushes the button and the engine roars to life. I fucking love cars, I'm not a girly girl like my sisters. I love engines and getting dirty. If I had my way there would be no college and I would be an appren-tice at a mechanic's shop learning to rebuild engines.

The radio plays softly in the background as he pulls out into traffic, the tension radiating between us so thick I can taste it on the tip of my tongue. I fucking hate him. He knows I hate him, so why the hell would he invite me back to his place to stay? How the hell does he know I have been staying in that rundown house, because I sure as fuck have never told him or anyone for that matter—I mean, it's not like I have any friends. Girls hate me because I'm too manly for them apparently, guys just want to fuck me, and since Jason, I have no interest in anything to do with the opposite sex. Corvin's phone rings through the Bluetooth of the phone and the name that flashes on the screen of the radio has me frowning.

He sighs before he hits decline on the steering wheel. The phone immediately starts to ring again, this time he answers. "What do you want, Darius?" he grits out.

"Hello to you too, asshole." I smirk, at least I'm not the only one who thinks he's an asshole then.

"Get to the point." Cody told me that Corvin was tight with his friends. She said they were as close as brothers, but the tone and the way he is tense next to me tells me a different story.

"Why the fuck do I have Troy cancelling a meeting with me in three weeks because of some fucking court case in North Carolina?" I swing my gaze to him and stare, he keeps his eyes forward and refuses to look at me.

"Some shit went down, I need him here. Find another lawyer," he clips out.

"See, I was going to do that but Goldie asked if you were in some type of trouble. Dear old Troy explained *you* weren't the one going to court but Alexa-fucking-Sutton is!" Darius's voice has risen now. "Why the fuck are you with Cody's little sister, Corv? That girl wants to murder you in your sleep and now she is in NC with you and—"

I cut Darius off. "Well, because we're fucking, duh." Corvin finally turns to me with wide eyes and his mouth hanging open. I wink and smack my lips together blowing him a kiss. Darius splutters on the other end of the phone and Corvin quickly ends the call before he can say anything else. I sit back in my chair and smile triumphantly.

"Why the fuck would you tell him that?" The indignation in his tone is clear but I don't give a shit. "Answer me, Alexa!" Hearing my name come out of his mouth does me in. I snap my gaze to him and make sure he can see the pure unfiltered hatred I feel for him in my eyes.

"Fuck. You." I grit my teeth and try to tamper the fury burning inside me. The prick just keeps his gaze forward and doesn't seem the least bit offended by my words.

"Been there, done that." His comeback has my eyes widening and me recoiling back into my seat huffing, that was never supposed to happen. The night before Cody's funeral I just needed to get away from everything, so I snuck out and went to a dive bar. I saw Corvin sitting there and had planned to fuck with him but then Jason walked in behind me. We argued, Corvin stepped in when Jason raised his hand and threw him out of the bar before the owner could. He bought me a drink to help me calm down. That drink turned into ten, then before I knew what was happening, we were laughing, then stumbling back to his motel where he fucked my brains out and made me come harder than I ever have before—granted, I've never actually come by the hands of another before him.

Guilt eats at me daily that I allowed myself to get distracted and fell into the trap that is Corvin Williams but never again.

We pull into the parking garage of his building and I marvel at it, this place is freaking huge! He parks the car and we both climb out, then he grabs my bags and carries them over to the lifts. I follow silently after him. The moment the doors open, we step into the small metal box and I wish I could say I was surprised when he pushes the lone 'P' for penthouse, but I'm not. The guy is loaded and has no problem showing off his wealth. He puts in a code on the little keypad and then the elevator begins to move. I make sure to keep a couple feet of space between us. I don't know what he's playing at here but I'll be damned if he catches me off my game again. The doors open and it takes more control than I want to admit to not allow my jaw to hit the floor, the opulent beauty of this place is awe-inspiring. It's like a magazine came to life. Chandeliers, white couches, paintings on the walls, art pieces on stands. I stumble after him, trying to take it all in. Floor-to-ceiling windows in the large living room that overlooks the city, the kitchen is just as impressive, with white marble counters, and stainless-steel appliances. I spy a spiral staircase, but he continues past the kitchen to a small hallway.

"Door on the right is the laundry, second on the left is the gym and this…" he says as he comes to a stop at the door at the end of the hallway and pushes it open, "… is your room for the time being." I stand in the doorway stunned as he enters and drops my meager possessions on the end of the bed. The room has the fluffiest carpet I have ever seen, solid dark wash dressers and side tables. The bed itself is huge, with a thick wooden headboard and footboard. "Closet is there," he says, pointing to a door I didn't see off to the side. He points to the one next to it. "That's the bathroom but the shower needs to be fixed so you'll have to use the one in my room." I'm too busy taking in the large space to notice he has moved and now stands a foot away from me. "I'll order some takeout and leave you to settle in." For a moment our eyes lock, I see all the different emotions swirling in the depths of his eyes, but the most prominent is wonder. Before I can ponder that thought any longer, he slips past me and closes the door quietly behind himself.

CHAPTER FOUR

Corvin

I lean against the counter frowning down at her as I watch her eat the Chinese food I ordered. The girl eats like a man and has no fucking class whatsoever, she is the total opposite to… I cut that train of thought off before I get sucked back into that pit of despair that seems to live inside me all the time. My phone rings, giving me a welcome distraction. I step away from her and move into the living room before accepting the call.

"Troy," I say in lieu of *hello*.

"Corvin, I managed to pull some strings and stroked the right egos, but you will need to make a hefty donation to the library they are rebuilding–"

I cut him off before he can keep drawing on. "So did you get it done?"

"Yes, you and Alexa have a meeting with the dean at Wake Forest University in North Salem on Monday morning. I don't know what the girl wants to major in so you need to sort that out, but everything else is in place. You'll need to cover both of your tuitions upon enrollment as well. All her papers have been sent over so they will be able to see she has graduated early."

"Thanks, Troy. I owe you one."

"Just keep her out of trouble for the next three weeks and then we should be fine."

"Will do," I say, then disconnect the call and gaze out the windows at the city view below. I love standing here and watching the world around me, it fascinates me to watch people and see just how different each of us is.

"Your room upstairs?" Alexa asks from behind me.

"Yeah."

"Can I use the shower?"

"Yeah," I answer, then turn around to tell her where the towels are but the words die in my throat. She stands there in a black bra and panties, her shirt and pants lay on the floor next to her feet. I'm too weak to stop myself from running my gaze over her exposed skin. Her body is perfection and sculpted like a masterpiece. The thin straps of her panties ride high on her hips, a belly ring gleams in the light, and her tits are practically overflowing in the cups of her bra. Before I can reach her face, I manage to find the strength and tear my gaze from her and stare back out the window. "Towels are in the closet beside the bathroom." My voice is gruff to my own ears. I listen to the soft sounds of her footfalls as she makes her way upstairs. I don't know what she is playing at and I have no fucking doubt this is a game to her, I just need to work out what her angle is.

Guilt churns inside me. I not only dishonored her sister by fucking her the night before her funeral but now I stand here with my cock rock-hard and pushing against the confines of my jeans just from the mere sight of her. I'm going to hell. I rest my head against the cool glass and close my eyes, imagining Cody and her contagious laughter, the girl always had a way of making me smile without even trying. I smile at the thought of her always putting me in my place or tearing me a new asshole when Leah and I would argue and she would insert herself in the debate just to back my sister up. Cody was loyal as fuck and I know her loss will be hitting my sister just as hard.

To distract myself from thoughts of Alexa, I slip my phone from my pocket and dial my sister. She picks up on the fourth ring. "Corv?" The surprise in her voice isn't lost on me, I don't talk to anyone anymore. I'm too scared they will finally figure out that I'm fucked up and leave me.

"Yeah, it's me," I mutter quietly. Silence stretches for a moment. Neither of us knows what to say to the other. I have barely said two words to my sister since I packed my shit and left. I couldn't be there anymore. CHU is a reminder of Cody, that house still sits there empty and no one has been in it since we all left. I know they are all waiting for me to go back and face it but… I can't.

"Is… is everything okay?"

A whoosh of air escapes me. "Not really, but it will be," I answer honestly.

"She wouldn't want you to be punishing yourself, she loved you—"

"I know!" I grit out and immediately regret snapping at her, it's not Leah's fault I'm such a fuck up. "I'm sorry. Shit is just… hard right now and I'm trying to… work through it." I can hear Darius saying something in the background but Leah shushes him, which brings a smile to my face. I never would have thought I would ever be okay with one of my best friends dating my sister, and I wasn't at the start, but seeing how much Darius loves her and would lay down his life for her without thought, shows me he is the perfect guy for my sister.

"Sorry, the halfback was being needy."

"Don't need to know that shit, Leah," I growl and she giggles.

"Sorry." Both of us remain silent for a beat and I hate that there is this bridge between us. I just don't fucking know how to cross it and get myself out of this rut. "Why is Cody's little sister staying with you, Corv?" she whispers.

"Straight to the point, huh?" She sighs so I quickly push on. "It was the right call. I fucked her life up, sis, it was the least I could do."

"You didn't do anything wrong, Corvin. You're punishing yourself for something you didn't do."

"If that's the case, then why are you and Darius in Chicago?" Her sharp intake of air has me cursing under my breath and a wave of guilt washing over me. I hear a scuffle on the other end of the phone and then Darius's voice booms through the phone.

"She may be your fucking sister, but you don't get to push your shit onto her. Feel me?" He doesn't give me a chance to answer. "We get you're fucking hurting, but you are the one who got your ass on a plane and ran the fuck off… You ran away to hide from this shit, Corvin. She needed her brother and you left her. Beck won't come back because you blame Val and it wasn't even her fucking fault. Saint and Crue are alone at CHU, picking up the pieces we all left behind. Did you know the board is trying to push them out or that Saint's dad is trying to force his hand and bring him home, because some cunt spread a rumor that he and Crue are fucking? Of course you wouldn't, because your head is so far up your own fucking ass right now!"

I open and close my mouth a few times but no words come out, I don't know how the fuck to answer him. Everything he said is right. I destroyed our family and I have no one to blame for that but myself.

"Don't say that to him!" I hear my sister shout in the background.

"Goldie, he needs to fucking hear it. I'm not gonna stand by and let this prick take it out on my girl because he's being a bitch." I scoff.

"A bitch? A fucking bitch, really?" I roar. "My girl fucking died because of Valance. If she had fucking dealt with that shit, that cunt would never have been at our house that day." I'm shouting now and my anger is suffocating me from the inside.

"She was a fucking hero, Corvin. She saved our nephew!" I slam my eyes closed and bang my head against the glass a couple of times, gritting my teeth to calm the hell down because as angry as I am, I know Darius is right.

"Both of you, stop it!" Leah shouts but Darius ignores her.

"Corvin, you are my best fucking friend, my brother in every sense of the word, but I won't sit by and watch you throw your fucking life away. Leah and I will be there next weekend. Don't argue about it, we need to bring this family back together."

"I have practice," I quickly add, trying to deter him.

"Cancel it!" Is all he says before he ends the call.

"Fuck!" I growl and spin around only to freeze on the spot at the sight of Alexa standing there in a towel with a murderous look on her face. My own slackens when realization dawns on me that she heard the conversation I just had. "Alexa—"

"Fuck you!" she screams and I flinch. "You don't get to stand there and talk about her like you gave a single fuck about my sister. She's fucking dead and it's all your fault."

I snap. "I know!" I roar so fucking loud she stumbles back a step. "You don't fucking think I know she's dead because of me?" I stalk toward her. She stands her ground and doesn't move an inch, even when I push into her, forcing her to crane her head back in order to meet my gaze. "Do your fucking worst, jail bait, as nothing you do to me can make me hate myself more than I already do." I turn and head upstairs to call it a night. I'm halfway up when her words have me slamming to a halt.

"She deserved so much better than you." I slowly turn back to face her and grip the railing in a vice like hold.

"Yeah, she did and I'll have to live with that for the rest of my life." I don't stick around, making a beeline for my room, ready to call it a night because if I don't, I'll find the nearest bar and find solace at the bottom of a bottle for a few hours.

Waking the next morning, I head into my closet and change into my workout shorts and a shirt. I kind of love this room because everything is open. My room takes up the whole second floor and it's fucking wicked that I have this entire space to myself. Once I'm changed, I head downstairs to the gym. I tiptoe down the stairs so I don't wake the demon at the end of the hall. I snag a bottle of water from the fridge and head for the gym. I push the door open and come to a stop. Alexa has her back to me as she runs on the treadmill in tiny spandex shorts that leave the bottom half of her ass cheeks out, and her hair is in a ponytail that swishes from side to side as she runs. She wears a sports bra on top and nothing else. Shaking my head, I tear my gaze away from her and move to the weight area. She doesn't spare me a single glance as I pass her.

I finished with the dumbbells, then move to the weight bench. Laying down, I brace my feet flat on the ground and reach up to grip the bar. Some say not having a spotter is a death wish but fuck it. I'm on the second set of ten when Alexa decides it's a fantastic fucking idea to straddle me. The bar wobbles in my hold and I push up to secure it back in its cradle, but the dirty little demon reaches out and presses down until the bar is flat against my chest. Gritting my teeth, I glare at her. She smiles wide at the sight of me struggling to breathe with this amount of weight on my chest.

"Alexa," I warn.

She bats her lashes and grinds down against my dick

causing it to twitch in my pants. "Corvin," she says in a sultry tone.

"What… are you doing?" I grit out as I push against her hold on the bar, but she leans forward, applying even more weight to it. My chest is fucking burning from lack of air.

"Showing you how easy it would be to end you, *Reaper*," she says in a sickly sweet tone before removing her hold on the bar. It's a struggle but I manage to return it to the cradle and drag in some much-needed air. She grinds down against my dick, but this time I don't let her win this little game. I move so fast she doesn't have a chance to escape. I grip her hips and sit up so my bare chest is pressed against her. The moment her eyes widen a fraction, I know I have the upper hand. I shift slightly so she can feel my hard length pressing against her pussy, drawing a gasp from her. Her eyes lock onto mine and as much as she tries to hide it, she can't. I see the lust lurking beneath the surface of her blue eyes. Her breath hitches as I bend down until we are eye to eye. My grip on her waist tightens, and the only indication she gives me that she is affected by my nearness is the slight twitch of her mouth. I hold her gaze as I ghost my lips over hers and say,

"I'd love to fuck with you some more, but you really are jail bait." Then I stand and fight the smile from breaking free at the sight of her falling to the ground and scowling up at me. I shoot her a wink as I say, "You want to kill me, better up your game, jail bait."

"Fuck you, Reaper," she seethes as I step over her, ready to stalk out of the room. The dirty little minx ankle taps me and I tumble face-first to the ground and only manage to stick my arms out at the last minute. I roll to my back, ready to have a go at her until her laughter pierces the air. The sound of it has me stilling and staring at her. Seeing her like this, uncaring and free of her anger for a minute, she really does look her age. Fuck. I shake my head and quickly climb to my feet and race from the gym, heading upstairs for a cold shower.

Not only is she my dead ex's sister, she is also under-fucking-age. I don't call her jail bait because I bailed her ass out, I call her that because I would go to prison for fucking her. If I wanted to make it to the NFL and anyone found out I was fucking a seventeen-year-old, my career would be over before it started. What the fuck is wrong with me? For weeks the thought of another woman disgusted me, but not even twenty-four hours with Alexa and already I've been hard twice and wanting nothing more than to sink my cock inside her again. Fuck, memories of the night with her at the motel assault me. Yeah, we were both drunk but you best believe your boy didn't suffer from whiskey dick and managed to fuck all night long. We each lost ourselves in the other. At the time, I had no idea she was using me as much as I was her. We both needed to escape our realities and we found that escape in each other's bodies. As much as I fucking enjoyed that night, I can't let it happen again.

CHAPTER FIVE

It's a Saturday night. I expected Corvin to have big plans and be heading out with friends or inviting some ho over to warm his bed, except he does neither of those. Instead, he sits on the couch in the living room watching ESPN in a pair of sweats and no fucking shirt. Does he not feel the freaking cold? I have no idea how long I stand here leaning on the kitchen counter watching him watch TV, but the moment my phone beeps with a text, I finally pull my stare from him, only to sigh at the sight of Jason's name. I click on the message and immediately wish I didn't.

JASON

North Carolina, huh?

How the hell does he know I'm here? I don't have to wonder that for long because another text comes through.

JASON

You forget, I know people, bunny.

I grit my teeth. I hate his stupid pet names for me. He's always called me sweet juice or bunny, because he says bunny rabbits are notorious for running away and my juices are sweet. I didn't run though, I broke up with his sorry ass having had enough of him using me as a punching bag. Jason used to treat me like a queen, but the moment he started snorting shit he changed. It was like he was a whole new person, gone was my attentive boyfriend who loved to cuddle and hang out. In his place was this new angry, hateful guy that blamed me for everything. If a guy smiled my way, I was a slut and would wind up getting thrown around the moment we got home. Cody hated him. My parents never cared enough about me to notice that I was sporting bruises or fractured ribs.

Not hiding shit and don't owe you an explanation for shit. We're done Jason. I told you that months ago so don't call me, text me or try and slide into my DM's again. Go to rehab and get your life back!

When five minutes goes past, I think he has given up on replying until my phone rings. Corvin doesn't move an inch, so I lull myself into thinking he isn't paying attention and decide to answer Jason's call, and end this back and forth once and for all.

"What?" I snap, low enough not to garner Corvin's attention, last thing I need is him putting his nose in where it doesn't belong. I fucked up this morning and I won't let him catch me slipping again.

"Sweet juice, don't fucking push me." I can already tell from the tone of his voice he's high. Jason comes from a wealthy family, which means he always has money at his fingertips to buy his next fix. His parents won't send him to rehab, there is no way Lauren and Kevin London would have the stain of their son needing to go to rehab on their perfect image. I turn away from Corvin and take a calming breath, knowing that this conversation will only end in him making threats that he'll find me and make me love him again.

"Don't call me that," I hiss. "I'm not pushing you, Jason. I'm telling you for the last time that there is no *us*, we are done."

"Why?" I close my eyes. Ever since Cody told me about her friend's stalker and the lengths that crazy bastard went through to get her, it woke me up to the fact that Jason is just as crazy as him. I went back to him every time because I had nowhere else to go. I knew if I had asked Cody she would have taken me in but she was in college and just starting her life, I couldn't burden my sister with that. The last time she and I made that promise to each other, I never went back. I went back to my parents for a while, until I couldn't handle the arguing with my mom every day and my dad telling me I wouldn't amount to anything. So I packed my shit and couch surfed for a while until I ended up here.

"Because I refuse to be on the receiving end of your fucking fists any longer. You need help, Jason, and I've told you this for a long time now–"

"I'm getting help, baby. I want you back. I'm nothing without you, Lexi." Before I can respond, the phone is ripped out of my hand. I spin around and stumble back a step at the sight of a red-faced Corvin, standing there with my phone against his ear.

"You motherfucker!" he growls down the phone. "You ever come near her again and I'll fucking kill you." He ends the call and tosses my phone onto the counter. His chest rises and falls in quick succession, his fists clench at his sides as he stares down at me.

"What the fuck do you think you are doing?" I shout.

"He laid his fucking hands on you?" he grits out through clenched teeth.

Shame washes over me and I dart my gaze away from him. He closes the space between us and pinches my chin between his fingers, forcing my gaze back to him.

"Answer me, jail bait." My nostrils flare.

"What the fuck is it to you if he did?"

"No man gets to lay his hand on a woman and hurt her–"

I scoff, cutting him off and shove against his chest but he doesn't shift an inch. "But you can break my sister's heart and that's okay?" I may not have been able to physically move him but my words hit hard. He stumbles backward until he smacks into the counter, staring down at me with an unreadable look on his face. "You don't get to butt into my business. You just fucking poured gasoline on that smoldering fire and now I'm gonna have to try to put it out again!" I make my escape, only to be yanked backward by my wrist. A hand wraps around my throat and then I'm slammed against the fridge. Corvin gets right in my face. I balk at him. Never once did Cody mention him ever getting handsy with her, so he has me at a disadvantage here.

"You ever have contact with that cunt you let between your legs again in my house, you will see a side of me your sister never got to." My eyes widen and before I can utter a single word, he stalks up the stairs leaving me standing here reeling. He comes back down, dressed in jeans and a sweatshirt and doesn't spare me a single glance, before storming toward the elevator and leaving me alone in his penthouse.

What the fuck just happened?

I pull my shit together after a few minutes and drag my sorry ass over to the sofa and drop down into it as I replay what the fuck just happened in my head, trying to make sense of Corvin's reaction to my ex. I scream in fright when my phone begins to ring in my hand. When I see who is calling, I decide at this moment the universe hates me! Before I can talk myself out of it and needing a distraction from what the hell just happened, I answer the call.

"What do you want, Katie?" I haven't spoken to her since the funeral, not through her lack of trying though.

"Alexa." She sounds surprised and I don't blame her. Half

the time I either let her calls ring out or send them to voicemail.

"Yeah?"

"Sorry, I'm just shocked you answered is all."

I roll my eyes. "Yeah, well, I'm just full of surprises, what do you want?"

"Just to check on you and see–"

"How I'm doing?" I don't give her a chance to respond. "Just fucking peachy. My best friend slash sister was murdered and I live with her ex fuck buddy who bailed me out of jail because I set his car on fire. So ya know, life is just fucking peachy." The sarcasm is thick in my tone but I give zero fucks.

"Wow, that's a lot." She laughs but it's forced. I remain silent, not having anything to say. She was Cody's best friend, not mine, and honestly, it pisses me off that they can all go on and live their lives while my sister is rotting in the ground. "Lexi, do you think living with Corvin is a good idea?"

Of course, it isn't but if I'm to destroy his life like I plan to then being here is the best place. "I mean, you already busted us fucking once, what more could happen?"

"Alexa, you're seventeen and he's twenty soon to be twenty-one. If you think something between you two can happen–"

I cut in before she can continue. "What I do is none of your business. Just go back to playing with the two dicks you have chasing after you and let me worry about myself, huh?" I don't wait for a reply and end the call, throw my head back and groan in frustration. Fuck everybody, them thinking they can tell me what to do. I've managed to do fine for myself all the time and I don't fucking need their pity or charity. I mean fuck, my own parents hopped on a plane two days after we buried Cody and flew to Thailand and never once asked me if I wanted to go. Shit, they haven't even called me since they left!

I'm about ready to turn the TV off and head to bed when my phone pings with an incoming text. I fight a groan, thinking it's Jason but frown when I see it's a message from Corvin. I open the thread.

REAPER

What size are you?

I balk at the screen.

Fuck off you perv!

REAPER

Coming from the girl who stripped in front of me last night and wanted to ride my cock this morning while trying to kill me?

You wish that strip show was for you! What do you want, Reaper?

REAPER

You never messaged me today….

I scoff, is he out of his damn mind!

I'm staying in YOUR penthouse, why the fuck would I text you?

REAPER

You've texted me every single day for the past six weeks at 11:42 every single day except today, why?

I reread his message at least four times stunned, yes I knew of course he would expect a text from me every day but I never realized he knew the exact time.

> What's the time got to do with it?

I wait anxiously for his reply wondering if he really knows what is so significant about that time.

REAPER

> It's the time they announced my heart stopped beating.....

> You mean the time they announced that my sister's heart stopped!

REAPER

> The moment they announced hers stopped beating, mine did too.

Without permission tears spring to my eyes as I read his message. It shouldn't affect me the way it does but I can't deny reading his words makes me feel a certain way. Disgust rolls through me. I slept with him when I never should have. Even if it meant escaping my reality for a few hours, I never should have found an escape in him—he's hers. Another message comes through pulling me from my thoughts.

REAPER

> Tell me something I don't know about her...

I want to deny him but truthfully, messaging him every day telling him something about Cody makes me feel closer to her. It's almost like she isn't really gone if we can keep her memory alive by speaking about her daily and not hiding the fact that she ever existed, like my parents are doing.

> When she was six she fell off her bike and knocked her two front teeth out on the concrete. It was on Easter weekend. That was her favorite holiday.

REAPER

crying face emoji You called her bugs that
weekend, didn't you?

Laughter burst out of me. I did call her Bugs, and her face
each time I said it was priceless. She wanted to hurt me but
she never did. No matter how mad I made her, Cody would
never do anything to hurt me. She was the best fucking sister
and here I am laughing at memories of her with the guy who
broke her heart and caused her death.

REAPER

Can I ask you something, jail bait?

No, you can't ask me anything. You've taken
everything from me, Corvin.

REAPER

You want to ruin me?

Yes, I want to watch you burn.

REAPER

You hate me?

Yes, more than anything in this world.

REAPER

The sight of me disgusts you?

I hesitate for a split second before I reply.

Yes.

REAPER

Good, I need you to hate me and look at me
like I'm nothing but the bane of your life.

Why....

REAPER

Because the sight of you doesn't disgust me and that's dangerous. Don't make the same mistake she did and find some low-life scum like me worthy of your time.

CHAPTER SIX

Corvin

I had to get the hell out of there earlier. Being that close to her and having my hands on her had me wanting to kiss her. I knew if I did that, she would kill me… but not only that, I couldn't do that to Cody. I ran away like a bitch. Darius was right, I do run from shit when it gets hard, which is why I drove around for hours until I found myself at the beach. I sat on the bonnet of my car, staring up at the night sky wondering if Cody could see me making a shit show out of my life. While I was there, I called the group chat I have with the guys for the first time in weeks. It was awkward for a bit, but then we slipped back into our old ways and talked shit for a long time. After that call, I started texting Lexi. I never should have sent that last message but I can't take it back. To get my head on straight, I go to my voicemail and click on the last message I got from Cody, the one where I rejected her call because I was a fucking prick.

"Corv, baby." The fear in her tone has me slamming my eyes closed and my heart aching inside my chest. The rest of the message plays out, and by the end of it, a lone tear trails down my cheek. I reply to the message and listen to it on a loop letting her voice lull me into a false reality where I can close my eyes and picture her face like I always do when I listen to it. Except this time, after the fifth time hearing the voicemail, it isn't her face I see behind my closed lids, it's Alexa's. I sit up so fast I slip off my hood and tumble to the ground on my knees.

"Fuck!" I growl out as I push myself to my feet, pocket my phone and jump in my car, then peel out of the lot, and head home, berating myself the whole fucking way! I'm a piece of shit. Here I am crying over the last voicemail from Cody and yet it's her fucking sister's face I'm picturing. I'm going to hell.

By the time I pull into the garage of my penthouse, it's after three in the morning. The moment the elevator doors shut, I slump against the wall as I recall I still need to tell the jail bait about her starting college on Monday and I can only imagine how well that is going to go. No doubt the crazy pyro is probably going to stab me or some shit! The moment the doors open my jaw unhinges.

"Motherfucker!" I roar as I march into my house, dodging bits of glass and broken pieces of furniture and art. I round the corner to see all the paintings on the wall are ripped and some look like she took a knife to them. I come to a halt between the kitchen and living room. The TV is smashed, plates and other various kitchen appliances are broken and scattered around the room. I march down the hallway and thank God that I locked the gym and the office doors this morning, so I continue on to her room. I throw the door open ready to rip her a new asshole but the fucking room is just as trashed as the rest of the house! I check the closet and the bathroom and find them empty. I begin to worry that someone might have broken in and my stomach bottoms out as dread pools in the pit of my stomach. "Alexa?" I scream as I race from the room and run up the stairs. I slam to a halt at the sight of her sitting in the middle of my bed with that tiny red box sitting in the palm of her hand. I looked and see no damage has been caused to my room except for the bedside drawer is open.

"You got this ring for her, didn't you?" I slowly walk toward her and drop down onto the side of the bed near her but keeping enough space between us. I stare down at the ring in her hand, it's an Emerald cut ruby and trapezoid, 18k, white gold diamond ring. Alexa slowly lifts her guilt-ridden gaze to mine, begging me without words to answer her.

"Yes," I whisper. She gasps, drops the ring and leaps off the bed, then stands in front of me. She strikes out and slaps me across the face.

"You couldn't even tell her you fucking loved her but you bought her a ring?" she screams. I don't touch my cheek to ease the sting, I just turn back to face her and wait for her to continue berating me. "You never deserved her!" she screams before slapping me again but this time I don't just take it, I snap my arms and grip hers. Then I yank her toward me and slam her on the bed, before climbing on top of her and pinning her arms above her head, while straddling her legs to keep her in place. "Get the fuck off me!"

I get right in her face until our noses are touching. "Shut the fuck up!" She stills beneath me for a tense moment then out of nowhere she fucking head butts me. Thanks to the close proximity the hit doesn't do shit, but it does stun me. "Calm the fuck down, you crazy little devil," I shout.

"Fuck you!" she screams so loud my ears ring.

"Not happening again, jail bait."

"I'd rather eat shit than let your dirty little cock near me again, Reaper." I frown.

"There is nothing little about my cock." Her eyes crinkle at the corners and fill with pure unfiltered hate. I never really realized how much she hated me until this moment.

"You are a coward." Those words have me tensing. "You buy a ring for my sister but can't even commit. You're pathetic and my sister was better off without you." Her words are like a bucket of ice water being thrown over me, I leap off.

"You may be right but we will never know. I won't let you throw away your life because you hate me. You start school with me on Monday." She opens her mouth to argue but I push on too tired to deal with her shit. "Shut the hell up, get your ass in the fucking bed and go to sleep, jail bait," I grit out before I turn and storm into my bathroom, slamming the door closed behind me. I grip the edge of the counter and take some deep breaths. Staring at myself in the mirror, I take a long hard look. The look I see in my own eyes is one I never wanted to ever see, defeat. I decide right now that I am going to do everything I can to regain control of my life and make something of myself. I won't let the loss of Cody weigh me down anymore. She wouldn't want that and I can't keep self-sabotaging.

Once I finish in the shower, I dry off and wrap the towel around my waist. I curse under my breath when I realize I didn't bring any clothes in here with me. Fuck it. I open the door and expect her to be asleep, low and behold I was fucking wrong. She sits crossed-legged in the center of the bed staring straight at me with her mouth slightly ajar and her eyes wide. Her eyes trek over my body and it's not lost on me when swallows audibly telling me she is affected by my presence. Her gaze lingers on my abs, and a smug sense of satisfaction washes over me when she shifts and squirms, I head for the dresser across the room feeling her gaze on me the entire way. Yanking the drawer open I pull out a pair of sweats and drop my towel, the hiss that comes from behind me has me fighting a smile from breaking free. I tug the sweats on and then turn to face the girl that is becoming an addiction I can't afford.

I pull my gaze from her, flick the light off, leaving the only light source in the room the bedside lamp. I ignore her as I climb in on my side, shut off the lamp and close my eyes. It's been a long emotional fucking day and I have to meet Travis tomorrow afternoon and train again. I feel her shifting on the bed but don't bother to open my eyes until she straddles my lap then my eyes are wide fucking open. I still beneath when I feel something pressed against my throat, neither of us says a word for a long while. When she makes no move to slit my throat open, I slowly reach out and turn the lamp on. Her eyes blaze with hatred—never in my life have I ever seen such a look on someone's face until now.

"It should have been you that died. You stole the only person in this fucking world that gave a shit about me. She would call me and tell me how amazing you are and how well you treated her but then after a while, shit changed. There wasn't this happy lilt to her voice anymore. I heard the pain each time she would talk about you and how you wouldn't commit to her. She envied her friends—Leah got her man, Katie got her guys and the worst was when she rang and told me the iceman of your friend group even got his girl and a kid. But still, you wouldn't just love her like she fucking deserved!" She presses the object in her hand harder against my windpipe, I can't see what the fuck it is. "Answer me," she screams, her eyes begin to fill with tears as she glares down at me and something about that broken look in her eyes pushes me over the edge.

I flip us so she's on her back and I hover above her, she keeps her weapon against my throat even as the first tear falls down her cheek. "I never lied to your sister, jail bait. She sought *me* out, not the other way around. Yes, it was supposed to be a one-night stand so no one caught feelings. When she came to me for more, I told her that I would never commit or be her boyfriend, this would strictly be sex and *she* agreed to those terms. Hate me all you fucking want but I never lied to Cody. Did I love her? Yes. Am I fucking sorry she was murdered because of me? Fuck yes, and I will live with that guilt for the rest of my fucking life because she never deserved that. I fucking tried to push her away but she wouldn't budge. She thought she could fix me, but she couldn't."

She frowns up at me, the pressure against my neck lessens slightly as she searches my gaze. "What do you mean *fix you?*"

"That's shit you don't need to know. Now either end my fucking suffering or get rid of that thing against my neck." She takes a shuddering breath, I see the war she is fighting within herself and decide to push her even further. "You'll never get another chance like this again, Alexa, so either take the shot or drop the fucking thing." Slowly she lowers the weapon and that's when I notice it's a broken piece of a vase. Nothing in here is trashed, she brought it up here with her. A sob slips past her full lips. Before I can even think of what to do next, my body takes on a mind of its own and the next thing I know my lips are pressed against hers. She tenses beneath me and I know without a doubt she is about to push me off, so I break the kiss and whisper, "Let me take your mind off the pain and you can go back to hating me tomorrow."

I don't wait for an answer before meshing my lips to hers. She drops the broken piece of the vase and wraps her arms around my neck, pulling me in closer, deepening the kiss. The moment the taste of her hits my senses, I groan. This is so fucking wrong but we both need this distraction to get the fuck out of our own heads. She scrapes her nails down my naked back pulling a moan from me. The moment she reaches my waistband, I pull back and sit on my haunches staring down at her. She sits up, holds my gaze as she grips my sweats and pushes them down enough to free my cock. It slaps against my abs—hard, angry and red. She darts her tongue out and tentatively grips me. I hiss at the feeling of her hand wrapped around my dick.

She pumps me twice before flicking her gaze back to mine. "This means nothing, it's just sex."

I nod my agreement. "Sure."

An evil glint enters her eyes as she continues to pump me as she speaks. "Don't get attached, don't ask for more because I'm not girlfriend material and believe me, I won't stop until I fucking ruin you." Before a reply can formulate in my mind, she wraps her luscious lips around my cock and sucks.

"Fuck, jail bait," I sneer. I feel her smile around my cock. The girl's mouth is like a fucking vortex and fuck me, she has no gag reflex. She takes my cock all the way to the back of her throat and moans, the vibrations sending a shudder through my body. If she keeps deep throating me like that, I'm gonna cum and like fuck is that going to happen. I grab a hand full of her hair, tug hard until she releases my cock with a wet pop and shove her back. I'm too fucking on edge to draw this out for her. I grip her leggings and yank them and her panties off, tossing them over my shoulder. She opens her legs wide, exposing her glistening cunt. Jesus Christ the hood of her cunt is pierced!

"Eat it or fuck it but don't fucking keep staring at it." I do as she commands and bury my face in her pussy. The second I push my tongue inside her tight wet hole, I growl my approval. She tastes so fucking good, I'm man enough to admit this is the best fucking pussy I have eaten. "Fuck, yes," she cries out as I continue to fuck her with my tongue. I switch and swirl my tongue around her clit before sucking it into my mouth. She bucks her hips off the bed and I'm stunned when she screams out she's coming. I've barely touched her and already she is exploding on my face. I've just learned that Lexi is so fucking responsive, I'm able to get her off in under a minute. I don't let her come down slowly, she deserves to be fucked hard after destroying my house. I grip my cock and line it up with her entrance. Her dazed gaze meets mine just before I slam balls deep inside her tight cunt. She cries out as I bury my face in the crook of her neck relishing in the way her pussy convulses and strangles the life out of my cock.

I give us each a few seconds to adjust before I brace my arms on either side of her face and push up so I'm hovering above her. Her blue eyes stare up at me with hunger, all the hatred she held in her eyes is gone for the moment as her body takes over and demands to feel the pleasure I'm inflicting on it. I pull almost all the way out of her before slamming inside her again. I do that a few more times before I sit back, grab each of her legs and rest them on my shoulders before pushing forward, so she is folded like a staple, and fuck her greedy cunt hard.

"Holy fuck, yes, fuck me just like that, Reaper." I ignore the fact that even when I'm buried deep inside her and making her feel something other than the pain she has been drowning in for weeks, she still calls me the bringer of death. I do as she says and fuck her hard. "Oh Jesus, I'm gonna come!"

She calls me Reaper but shouts the lord's name, go figure.

Her pussy clamps down on my cock, milking it for everything it's worth. Like a pubescent teen that hasn't fucked before, I'm powerless to stop my own body from coming with her. I throw my head back and roar out my release that is so fucking powerful, full body shudders wrack my entire frame. I push her legs off my shoulders and slump forward onto her, breathing heavily. The only sounds that can be heard in the entire room are our labored breaths. Neither of us says a word until my cock twitches when she shifts and reality crashes down on me. I push up and stare down at her in horror.

"Are you on the pill?" She frowns for a second, then her

eyes shoot wide. She shoves against my chest forcing me back. I pull out of her and hate that she flinches. I was too fucking rough with her. She swings her legs over the side of the bed and races to the bathroom while I stay motionless and stare after her.

CHAPTER SEVEN

Alexa

I yank my shirt over my head and rid myself of my bra tossing it to the side before I step into the shower stall and turn it to cold hoping the cold spray will shock me out of my moment of stupidity. I stand directly under the shower head shivering, but not feeling the bite of the cold. How the fuck did I just let that happen? I scrub my hands down my face and growl, I'm a fool. I reach out for the body wash and begin to scrub my body to rid it of the feeling of his touch until I reach my pussy. I can still feel him inside me, the way his cock stretched me open. Even with the shower freezing cold I start to get hot at the thought of how easily my body responded to him.

"Fuck," I rasp out, needing to get my head on straight. Trashing his apartment was my way of showing him how much I hate him and don't care for anything except causing him pain, but the moment I came up here to trash his room, I found that fucking ring. The sight of it threw me into a pit of grief. I don't understand how he cannot commit to her, yet he can buy her a fucking ring and never give it to her. Cody loved him, she told me so herself. I remember when she rang me on Christmas Eve and told me she finally told him she loved him. I was so happy for my sister until she broke down and said he never said it back and just walked out on her.

The bathroom door flies open and I scream in fright. Corvin stalks toward me naked and uncaring, then steps into the stall with me, not even bothered by the freezing temperature of the water. He grips the back of my neck and hauls me forward forcing me to place my hands against his naked chest to keep a sliver of space between us. Bending at the knees, he gets right in my face, his light brown eyes shine with a look I can't decipher. He grips my waist with his other hand and holds me in place. I hate that my body hums with awareness at how close he stands to me and the fact he is naked doesn't fucking help. To make it worse, I know all too well how amazing he fucks. That thought has my pussy fluttering, my dirty cunt literally just fluttered at the memory of how amazing his cock felt inside me.

"I fucked up. I'm sorry," he grits out.

"Sorry for what exactly, *Reaper?*" His left eye twitches at my name for him, but that's the only reaction he gives me.

"I never should have fucked you without a condom. I lost my head and that is my bad. I never should have fucked you, again."

I snort. "Well, look at you all apologetic and shit." I harden my stare as I look at him. "Let's get one thing straight, *you* never fucked me, *I* fucked you, there is a difference."

His upper lip pulls back in a snarl. "It was still my name you were screaming minutes ago."

I grit my teeth and hate that he is able to throw that shit back in my face. Taking back control of this situation, I run my hand down his sculpted chest and love the way he eyes me with apprehension but yet he still doesn't stop me. I reach his cock and fight the gasp that wants to break free when I find him hard already. A self-satisfied smirk graces his face and I want to knock it off. Wrapping my hand around the base of it I squeeze and slowly pump, loving that pained hiss that comes from him. I lean forward and nip at the side of his neck before licking a trail to his lobe.

"You like that?" I whisper huskily as I continue to pump him at a steady pace.

"Fuck, yes." I smirk triumphantly and quickly drop his cock before gripping his balls in my hand and squeezing hard. He screams like a little bitch. I use my hold on his balls to push him backward until his back is flush against the tiled wall. He stands there with his hands raised as if surrendering, breathing hard and fast. "Let. Go," he grits out, the pain is evident in his voice.

"You're going to answer a few questions first," I snarl and increase the pressure on his nuts, forcing him onto his tiptoes.

"Fucking ask whatever you want you crazy pyro," he shouts.

"Why'd you buy the ring?" When he takes too long to answer, I twist his balls and he screams so fucking loud I almost feel sorry for him.

"I bought it after she died!" he roars. My face slackens and I relent a little and don't crush his balls as tightly, allowing him a moment to breathe a little easier.

"Why?"

"She told Katie about the ring and said it was her dream wedding band. After she died, I couldn't bear the thought of someone else having that ring so I bought it." I should be livid, cursing him out or ripping his balls off but I don't do any of those things. I just stand here and stare up at him for a long while.

"You were telling the truth earlier, weren't you?" I utter.

"About what?" he snaps.

"You told her from the start you would never love her." He takes a shuddering breath and closes his eyes as he nods. After a second, he spares me with those brown eyes.

"I never lied to her, Alexa." The truth of his words can be heard.

"But you never let her go either," I sneer. "I'm going to fucking ruin your life, I have to." A defeated sigh escapes him.

"I know. Which is why I won't stop you, press charges or do anything to fuck up your life."

"Why?" I ask skeptically.

His gaze bores into mine. "Because it's what she wanted."

I slept like shit next to Corvin. I stuffed pillows in the middle of the bed to make sure he didn't cross onto my side. I would have slept downstairs in the room he gave me but it was destroyed. The moment the sun was out, I was up and dashing from his room. Last night was a mistake that I won't be repeating again. The second I saw the carnage downstairs, I actually felt like an asshole but what can I do about it, the damage is done. I do decide to be a good bitch and clean up my room so I won't have to sleep with Corvin again but fuck, I did a good job of fucking shit up.

"Alexa!" The sound of him shouting my name rouses me from my thoughts. I look around my room and cringe. I've been in here for hours and it still looks like shit. Fuck it. I leave the room and go in search of Corvin only to find him standing in the living room with an older looking guy in a suit. Corvin is red faced and looks like he might stroke out if he doesn't calm the fuck down. He says nothing, just stands there and continues to glare at me. I grow tired of waiting so I speak.

"What? You scream for me then stand there like a fucking mute." His nostrils flare in anger. He snakes his arm out and holds it directly in front of my face. I frown at all the text messages from random numbers. I peer around the phone and quirk a brow at him. "Uh, you're popular, cool."

His eyes narrow to slits. "You fucking little shit. Troy just informed me that you blasted my number on Craigslist." Oh shit, I can't help the laughter that bursts out of me. I'm laughing so hard that I wind up hunched over, gasping for air with tears trekking down my cheeks. "What the fuck?" he snaps, ruining my moment. I stand up straight and roll my eyes.

"I told you, just because we fucked didn't mean I would stop fucking with you." His upper lip pulls back in a snarl and the guy Troy coughs to mask his laughter.

"Why are fucking dudes messaging me and saying they accept my offer for a room?" I smile wide and bat my lashes up at him as I answer.

"I may have put an ad out saying I needed somewhere to live, I couldn't afford to pay rent so I offered them my pussy as payment but don't worry, I didn't post a picture of myself on there." As crazy as it seems he looks relieved by that but I'm not done. "I used a picture of your sister." That does it, he takes a single step and then I'm off running. I hear him behind me and decide to avoid the mess of my room and race up the stairs to his to lock myself in the bathroom. He's so fucking close I can practically feel his breath on the nape of my neck. I reach the landing and take one step before I'm ankle tapped and sent sailing forward, before I can smack face first into the carpet I twist and land on my side. He looms above me, looking like he wants to wring my neck, I may be fucked in the head because rather than being terrified that he may hurt me, I'm thrilled at the prospect of seeing how far I can push before he really does snap.

"You are going to pay for that little stunt," he pushes out past clenched teeth. I rest up on my elbows and smile up at him which only serves to piss him off further.

"Look, in my defense I thought I was helping you out," I say sweetly.

"How the fuck would guys offering to fuck me help?"

I shrug my shoulders. "I figured having a dick in your ass

might loosen the stick you have up there twenty-four-seven." His eyes blaze with anger. I bite my bottom lip to keep from laughing. He crouches down beside me, clearing his face of all anger and replacing it with a look of... need which throws me off kilter. He reaches out and runs his fingers through my long raven hair, his tender touch has me on edge.

"Oh, jail bait." He tsks me and I tense, something isn't right. He's supposed to be pissed and going off the deep end, not looking at me like this. "If you thought the idea of having a cock in my ass would send me into a fit of rage, then you're not as smart as you thought you were." My jaw unhinges, drawing a chuckle from him. "One of my best friends is in love with the other one, I have no issues with embracing my sexuality."

"What?" I screech, earning a wicked smirk from him.

"Oh, baby, thing is I'm not pissed at you about this, I'm actually kind of impressed at the lengths you are willing to go through." I swallow waiting for him to deliver the punchline that I know is coming.

"But?" I push earning a wink from him.

"You know you have to deal with Darius when I tell him you used his girlfriend's picture on an ad offering sexual favors and believe me, I'm the nice one out of the two of us." I feel like I should be worried, but I'm not. Darius means nothing to me and it's not like I'm ever going to see the guy. "I can't wait to see your face when we catch up with them at the cabin for Easter—"

"What the fuck?" I cut in.

He just smirks and shrugs his shoulders. "See, before your little stunt interrupted things. Troy was here to tell me he managed to get your case thrown out on the terms you agreed to probation–which of course you did." I balk at him. "You also have to do community service for a couple of months. We managed to get the courts to agree to allow you

to complete your service on campus cleaning the workshops."
Everything else he said flees my mind.

"Workshops?" He nods. He thinks he's delivered me the worst news in the world, but in truth, this is the best news I have gotten since losing my sister.

"Deal."

He scrunches his face in confusion. "What?"

"I said deal, I'll do it." He eyes me warily, clearly sensing something is up.

"Why aren't you fighting me on this? I just told you that you're spending Easter with me and my friends, you have to stay here and you also have to clean the workshops on campus."

"I'm not like my sister, I don't do dancing and girly shit. Cleaning the workshops on campus means I get to fuck around with engines and tools. That's my jam, so I guess I should thank you." He pins me with a surprised look.

"You want to be a mechanic?" Out of nowhere the feeling of shame that always accompanies me when I tell someone what I want to do with my life rears its ugly head. This is what happens when you have a father and mother that tell you for years that this is a man's world and a woman working in a male predominant industry isn't right. I expect him to laugh and say the same thing as my parents when I nod my confirmation and drop my chin to my chest. A growl comes from him before he's gripping my chin and forcing my gaze back to his. I don't see doubt or laughter in his eyes as I expected. "Why are you hiding?" I shrug instead of answering, earning an annoyed sigh from him. "You steal my car, burn it out, smash it to pieces, trash my house and nearly rip my balls off and don't get embarrassed over that, but the fact you want to work on cars does?"

I huff out a laugh, he isn't wrong. "It's stupid I know—"

"No, it's not. Who the fuck says it is?" I try to look away

again, but his hold on my chin hardens, keeping me in place to answer him.

"My parents, okay? I'm not like my sisters and want to be a housewife, go shopping every fucking day and spend money like it means nothing. I want to work, fix cars and eventually build my own and earn a living. Don't fucking judge me," I snarl, my defenses are up high now, I don't care if he laughs at me because one day I will fucking do it and prove them all wrong.

"Well your parents are dicks." My eyes bulge. "I think that's fucking cool. I know my opinion doesn't mean shit but for it's worth, I think that is wicked that you know what you want from life. You have a meeting with the dean tomorrow after me, you'll start school in the fall here in North Carolina. Until then, I'll see what I can do about getting permission for you to sit in on some classes until then." I sit here stunned fucking speechless, I don't know what to say. "All your tuition will be covered, you won't have to worry about that or your accommodation, I'll cover it all." I stare at him with my mouth open and at a loss for words. He releases me and climbs to his feet. He turns to head back downstairs but my words stop him.

"Why are you doing this?" He keeps his back to me as he answers.

"Because I want to help you. I have the means to do it so why not?" He turns to peer down at me over his shoulder. "I also don't expect you to fuck me to pay your rent." I snort as he laughs, then makes his way back downstairs to Troy.

I lay back on the carpet and close my eyes as I let myself absorb what he just said. He didn't laugh at me or even try to steer me on a different path, he actually encouraged me and said he would pay for my schooling. My father refused to pay for it and said to get scholarships to cover everything because he wouldn't support a daughter who was only setting herself up to fail.

CHAPTER EIGHT

Corvin

Alexa and I have spent the whole day cleaning up the mess she made. No matter how much shit we pick up, there just never seems to be an end in sight. At around eight I call it quits and told her to order something from the menus in the drawer while I make a call to get someone to come clean this fucking place tomorrow while we're out. I also need to get someone to deliver groceries since she threw everything out of the fridge and now it's spoiled. The girl doesn't even seem like she feels guilty for destroying my house. Truth be told, I bought the penthouse fully furnished, so none of this shit I was emotionally attached to.

The girl probably did me a favor by trashing the place, but I won't tell her that. I'll make some calls tomorrow and have someone come out and redo the whole fucking penthouse. Walking into the kitchen, I don't see her so I head down the hallway toward her room and stop when I hear her speaking on the phone with someone, in a hushed tone.

"I said no. Don't come out here." She pauses as she listens to what the other person is saying. "I don't give a shit, we're done and you're a junkie that needs fucking rehab. We were good together until you thought it was a good idea to use my fucking face as a punching bag, Jason." My restraint snaps, I barge into her room. Ignoring the shocked gasp that slips from her, yank the phone out of her hold, then bring it to my ear.

"I'm coming and there isn't anything you can do to stop me!" The cunt seethes. I keep my angry glare on the defiant firecracker in front of me as I speak.

"She may not be able to stop you but I will. You step a single foot in North Carolina, you scummy piece of shit, and it will be my hands beating your fucking face for fun." I end the call and shove her phone in my pocket. That seems to be the thing that snaps her out of her stupor.

"What the fuck, I told you to stay the fuck out of my shit, asshole!"

"I told you never to speak to that cunt again in my house," I shout back. "I warned you there would be consequences."

"Fuck you and fuck your stupid ass–" I don't allow her to finish before I wrap my hand around her throat and glide her across the room until she smacks against the wall with a grunt. Fire burns in the depths of her eyes as she scowls up at me.

"I told you that you would see a side of me that your sister never got to meet if you defied me," I growl in her face. I expect her to fire back at me but as per usual with this girl, she surprises me when the anger in her eyes slowly bleeds way to... want. I know this is a bad idea, the worst fucking idea, but I can't seem to care that she is only seventeen and could land my ass in a jail cell. "Get on your knees," I grit out. I'm taking a huge risk here after what she did last night to my balls, but my cock is already hard and begging to be buried inside her again. I release my hold on her neck. We stand here, glaring at each other, waiting for the other to crack and admit defeat first.

"That what you want?" She runs her dainty little hands up my arms causing goose flesh to erupt along my skin. "You want me to suck your cock and swallow every drop of cum you give me?" Fuck. The husky lilt of her voice and the look on her face has my breathing accelerating and my cock twitching in my pants at the mental picture she has just painted for me. I know without a doubt that she is going to do something that will leave me in pain so I get the upper hand while I can and lean down brushing open-mouthed kisses along her neck relishing in the way her breathing stutters. I flick my tongue out and lick her ear enjoying the way her body presses into me. Fucking got you now, jail bait.

Ghosting my lips over her ear I whisper, "I wouldn't trust your scheming ass to suck my cock without biting it." She gasps and shoves me but I don't budge.

"Go fuck yourself, Reaper," she sneers, and I take a step back, wink at her, before turning and leaving her standing there to fume on her own. Halfway down the hallway, I smile to myself knowing that she is going to be fucking pissed.

Motherfucker!

I stumble forward when something hits me in the back of the head, and before I get a chance to right myself and turn around, something else hits me in the back. "What the fuck?" I shout as I turn around and wish to fucking God I hadn't when I see the hardback book coming at me. I'm too late to cover my face. The moment it smacks me in the nose I'm off my feet and on my ass, cursing that fucking devil that stands in the doorway smiling while I sit here with blood dripping down my fucking face. "The fuck is wrong with you?" I shout.

She saunters slowly toward me with a smile that rivals Lucifer's. "You. You're what's wrong with me. You treat me like a child and take my phone but want me to suck your cock?" I expect her to stop and keep space between us but like I said, she's full of surprises. She stands over me and doesn't stop until my face is in line with her pussy. Reaching down, she grips a handful of my hair and wrenches my head back to meet her gaze. "See, I think we can make this little arrangement work." I search her gaze, trying to figure out what angle she is working here because I know for sure she is up to something.

"What arrangement?"

She lowers herself down to her knees and straddles my lap—instantly my cock is hard and straining against the confines of my pants. She grips the collar of my shirt and brings it up to wipe away the blood, while I sit here with my hands at my sides, tense as fuck, waiting for her to deliver her next blow. Once she's finished cleaning the blood, she smiles and rests her hands on my shoulders. You know in horror movies when the crazy stalker ex-girlfriend comes in and makes an offer too good to refuse but you know the guy is a dumbass because he'll agree? I feel like that dumbass knowing this girl is going to fuck me six ways to Sunday.

"Let's call a truce." My brows jump to my hairline.

"A *truce*?" I practically screech. "With who?"

She rolls her eyes. "Between me and you, silly." Oh fuck, she's going to kill me. "No more silly little pranks until after community service."

"Are you high?" She frowns down at me. "Seriously, are you fucking high because *you* are the one who has been fucking with *me*. You stole my car, burnt it, trashed my house–" She places her index finger against my lips and shushes me.

"Don't dwell on the past, babe, let's move forward and call a truce. I mean, we have a meeting with the dean tomorrow and you're gonna need me to help cover the bruise that's already forming on your face."

I scoff. "Because you threw a fucking book at me!" I shout.

She rolls her eyes and sighs dramatically. "Would it make you feel better if I fucked the pain away?" I swallow loudly, clamp my mouth closed and shake my head. "Hmm, see I would believe you, but I can feel how hard you are beneath me." Jesus Christ, it's like she has a direct line to my cock because the fucker twitches and she smirks triumphantly. I watch like a stunned fucking circus clown with my mouth open as she stands and pushes her leggings and panties down her legs, she rids herself of her shirt and bra.

"Fuck." The one word tumbles from me without consent as I sit here and stare up at her. She's fucking beautiful. I'm so fucking hard just from the sight of her, I've never been like this before. Fighting with Cody never got me hard, if anything it would take her on her knees blowing me after a fight to get me going but with Alexa, fighting seems to be a default setting with us and that shit has me rock hard in seconds. She straddles me again but shifts down my thighs so she can undo my jeans, the moment she frees my cock it smacks against my stomach. She reaches out and grips my cock, drawing a hiss from me, then wraps both her hands around my length and begins to pump me. Fucking hell, this feels so good. I drop my head back and groan.

"Do we have a truce?" she asks huskily. I lift my head and meet her gaze, knowing what I should say. We both are still grieving and this whole situation is fucked up and shouldn't be happening, but how the fuck can I deny her when she is jerking me off and sitting on my lap stark fucking naked, ready to be fucked? I must take too long to respond. She shuffles forward and lines my cock up with her entrance while pushing her tits right in my face. "Say yes and I'll ride your cock until you're screaming *my* name."

Fuck it, we all gotta die someday.

I lean forward and suck her nipple into my mouth, loving the scream that rips out of her. Gripping her waist, I hold her in place as I slam inside her. We both cry out in ecstasy. I release her nipple with a wet pop and look up at her, the blissed-out look in her eyes has me wanting to puff out my chest.

"Don't burn any more of my cars or trash my house again

and you got a deal." She doesn't use words, she leans down and captures my lips in a kiss that robs me of air, whilst grinding down on my cock and riding me like a fucking porn star. She breaks the kiss. Resting her forehead against mine, she holds my gaze as she continues to drive us both insane with her slow rocking motions. This is a first for me, I've never fucked a chick and maintained eye contact before. Most girls try to hide or close their eyes, but not Alexa. She wants me to see it's her fucking me, making sure she is the sole focus of my attention.

This girl is fucking dangerous. She isn't like any of the other girls I've ever met—fuck, she isn't even like her sister. Cody was shy and would never fuck from the front if it was light out, it was always doggy style or reverse cowgirl. A moan tumbles from Alexa, drawing me back to the present. I hold her stare and watch transfixed as her eyes show me everything without the need to speak the words. Call me crazy, but being this close to her and staring into her eyes has me feeling like this is more than sex and that scares the fuck out of me. Needing to break free of this spell she has me under, I wrap an arm around her waist and use my other hand to push to my feet, she wraps her arms and legs around me with my cock still buried deep inside her cunt.

I shuffle forward with my pants still around my ankles and slam her against the wall, not giving her a chance to speak or question my motives. I grip her ass and hold her in place as I draw back before slamming inside her, loving the cry that tears from her. I take my frustration and lack of self-control out on her body. I'm ruthless in how I fuck her, not caring that my grip on her ass will leave bruises. A sick part of me wants to mark her, so I do. I lean forward and suck the soft flesh of her neck into my mouth and bite down relishing the cry she lets out.

"Fuck, just like that." I keep to the same pace, needing her to come all over my cock, to feed the monster inside me that wants to own her. "Corvin!" she screams, right as her tight little pussy clamps down on my cock milking it. She goes limp in my arms as I continue to slam into her harder, chasing my own release. The moment I feel my balls begin to tighten, I pull out of her, shove her to her knees, and grip my cock in my hand pumping it twice.

"Fuck," I roar out as jets of cum spurt all over her face and tits. Utterly fucking spent, I reach out and rest my hands on the wall above her, breathing hard and fast. I startle the moment I feel her hand wrap around my cock. I'm ready to jump out of her reach, thinking she is about to rip it off for coming on her like I did. Before I can do any of that, a moan tears out of me when she wraps her lips around my cock. "Oh fuck," I breathe out, shudders rolling through me. Fuck! Looking down at her on her knees, with my cock in her throat, is a sight to behold. She pulls back after a second and lifts her gaze to mine. The look in her eyes steals my breath, I see it right there just beneath the surface. This truce is a ploy, I know it, she knows it and now I just need to figure out what she has planned for me.

CHAPTER NINE

Alexa

The tension between Corvin and me is at an all-time high and being in the car with him makes it almost impossible to breathe without choking on it. I know last night was a bit much for him but I had to do it in order for him to let his guard down and agree to my terms. We both showered and crawled into his bed. Not a word was spoken, but waking this morning was awkward as we were both wrapped around each other. You best believe I jumped out of bed and called the first shower just to get away from him. I kept my word and helped cover the small bruise on his face—it'll be gone within a day or two at the most. I need him to let me in and let his guard down, which is why I'm about to do something I never thought I would. This is the only way I know how to get revenge for my sister.

Taking a deep breath, I force the words out. "Cody's death wasn't your fault." The car swerves and he quickly rights it before looking at me with disbelief clear on his face.

"Say what now?" I roll my eyes and turn to look out the window brushing him off, I won't say it again. It was fucking hard saying it the first time. "Alexa, as much as I would love to think I fucked the hatred out of you, not even I'm stupid enough to believe my cock is that magical." I snort and bite down on my lip to keep from laughing.

"Just drive, Reaper, you heard me fine and I won't repeat it." I don't even have to see him to know he is smiling at me, and the second I feel him pull his gaze from me, I deflate. Saying those words aloud was fucking hard but I had to say it. I need to make him believe it in order for this plan to work.

Corvin leads the way to the administration building. I'm falling behind but I can't find it within myself to care because this is fucking amazing. I've visited CHU but it didn't look like this, the buildings are old and spaced out. Wake Forest University has a welcoming type of feel to it. The quad is filled with students milling about or heading to their first class of the day. Not watching where I'm going, I smack into someone. I stumble back but he snakes his arms out to grip my waist to keep me from falling.

"Hey, you good?" I look up and smile, my savior has *stunning*, green eyes, sandy blond hair, and a smile that could melt the panties off any woman.

"Yeah, I'm good now," I say with a flick of my brows earning a laugh from him. He drops his hold on me and takes a step back. "What's your name?"

He chuckles and shakes his head. "Ash, but I can already tell you are trouble." I shoot him a toothy smile, I like this guy. The moment is shattered when I feel Corvin press up against my back. Ash looks from me to him and shakes his head clearly reading between the lines. "Nice to meet you, trouble."

"See you round, Ash," I call out as he walks off with his friends. The smile drops off my face when I feel Corvin's lips graze my ear.

"Your desperation is showing, jail bait." My jaw unhinges,

and I spin around to give him a piece of my mind, except the fucker stalks off toward the admin building, leaving me no choice but to follow after him like a lost fucking puppy!

The moment Corvin gives the receptionist our names, she leads us through to the dean's office, tells us to take a seat and leaves. I drop into the stupid leather chair in front of the desk and cross my arms over my chest, pissed off. I spy Corvin out of the corner of my eye dropping into the other chair beside me. I want to fucking smack him. How dare he call me desperate! I mean, he isn't wrong. I am fucking him so clearly I am scraping the bottom of the barrel. I'm pulled from my thoughts when the door opens and a man with salt and pepper hair wearing a suit that looks too big for him enters the room. He smiles kindly at us, then rounds the desk and sits down.

"I'm Laurence Moss, I'm the dean of admission here at WFU," he says with a smile.

"Thank you for seeing us on such short notice," Corvin replies, sounding like a posh prick.

"Of course, Mr. Williams. I must say, we were surprised that you would transfer here, not that our team isn't great or anything, but with only a short amount of time left before you graduate, I would have thought a player as accomplished as yourself would have wanted to finish out with his starting team."

Corvin tries to hide his unease, but I can see it clear as day on his face. "I needed a change and was told that WFU was looking for a starting QB after yours was taken out by injury." I tune them out as they discuss everything sports and what Corvin will have to do in order to get on the team and earn the starting position. Peering out the window of Laurence's office, a pang of guilt hits me. Is this how Cody felt when she first enrolled in CHU? I wonder if she knew then that she would never graduate or make it through her freshman year. I close my eyes and will those thoughts away. I need to be strong in order to do this, if he sees me crumble all of this will be for nothing.

"Miss Sutton?" I shake my head and turn to Laurence smiling sheepishly.

"Sorry, I got lost in my head." He smiles politely but I can tell it's forced.

"Mr. Williams has supplied us with your transcript papers and the… court order." I flinch at the reminder of my community service requirements. "WFU is willing to agree to allow you to complete your court order here but unfortunately, our classes are full until next year." Hope flees me and I slouch back into my seat feeling defeated.

"No, that wasn't the deal!" Corvin snaps, drawing the dean's attention back to him. "She starts with me or I pull my donation and you go against CHU without a QB and someone who has inside information that will get you to the finals. Your choice." I stare at the side of his head in shock.

"You would be throwing away your career here, no other school will take you this late in the year."

Corvin doesn't let him finish speaking. "You have my terms. You get her into the workshop as a student so she can study mechanics or I back out. Which will it be?"

Corvin and I walk out side by side. I have no fucking idea what the hell I should say. The guy put his career on the line for me, I never fucking saw that curve ball coming! Laurence agreed to Corvin's terms, which shocked me further. I mean, I knew they were all rich and somewhat powerful but I had no idea just how powerful they are, or the fact they own half of CHU is mind fucking blowing!

Maybe I am in over my head.

If he is able to get a court to change my community service and get my court case dropped, I should have clued in then just how well connected he is. He unlocks the car and slips behind the wheel. I slip inside and close the door, waiting for him to start the car. When he doesn't, I look over at him to find him staring straight out the windscreen with a blank look on his face.

"Your tuition is paid for, I also paid the next three years' worth of your tuition as well." My eyes widen to the size of saucers and my mouth drops open. "They'll have a dorm room for you within the next couple of weeks, all your living expenses will be covered."

"What is it you said to me, as much as I would love to believe I fucked some humility into you, even I know my pussy isn't that good." He slowly turns to face me, the pained look in his eyes throws me for a loop. "Why are you doing this?" I whisper.

"Because you were right, your sister deserved better than me. I couldn't give her that so the least I can do is make sure that you do better than me." Why the fuck do his words have a pang of regret hitting me in the chest. "I'll get you everything you need for your dorm, all your books will be covered." I open my mouth but no words come out, I just sit here and stare at him in shock. "I know this doesn't change shit Alexa, I'm not stupid. You're smart, really fucking smart and starting college early. Don't let a fuck up like me ruin your chance at a better life. Live your life and have fucking fun."

"Fun?" I rasp out. "How the hell am I supposed to do that when my sister is—"

"By living for the both of you!" he cuts in and says, "Don't do it for anyone but yourself. Your sister wanted the world for you, and if I can help make that wish come true, I will."

I eye him skeptically. "How would you know that?" He takes a shuddering breath then shakes his head and starts the car. "Answer me," I demand.

He puts the car in drive and keeps his gaze ahead as he

answers me. "Because she told me." I just sit here and stare at him as he drives us back to his penthouse. He paid for my schooling without me begging or pleading or even asking him to. He never questioned my choice of career or told me to aim higher, just agreed and said it was cool. He fought for me today and I don't know how I feel about that. No one has ever fought for me the way he did today, not even Cody.

We're halfway back when I finally ask, "You're really going to let me live in the dorms?"

He scoffs. "Jail bait, I won't *let* you do anything. You'll do what the fuck you want when you want. I know you living with me isn't ideal. I'll have Troy check with the courts to make sure you won't be breaking anything by moving, but I doubt you will since the case was dropped."

"So, after everything I've done to you… you're just going to pay for my school and housing and that's it?"

He sighs and nods. "Yes. I don't expect anything from you."

"What happens when I'm lonely in my dorm room and want you to fuck me?" He chokes on air, laughter bursting out of me at his reaction.

"Har-Har, shithead!" he deadpans.

Once my laughter is under control, I push him again. "So, is that a no to fucking me?" He flicks his gaze to me and I gasp, his eyes are filled with heat and need for… me.

"Something tells me even if I did say no, you wouldn't listen." I smirk as he focuses back on the road again. A couple minutes of silence passes before he speaks again. "I'm not stupid, Alexa. I know this truce you called last night isn't because you're over anything or forgive me." I tense in my seat and keep my gaze focused out the window. "If fucking me is what makes you feel better, then fine, do it. If hurting me makes you happy, hurt away. If the need to destroy me is what you seek then keep doing what you're doing, because soon enough you'll have that power over me."

I snap my gaze to him, and for a split second when our eyes connect, there are no masks, no pretense or fake agendas. We let the other see inside us and without meaning to, I see it inside Corvin's, he's telling the truth. He's falling for me and he hates himself for that, but I can also see that a larger part of him doesn't give a shit. He's willing to fall for me even though he knows I'm going to destroy him.

CHAPTER TEN

Corvin

Alexa says nothing the rest of the drive home. Not even when we walk inside the penthouse. I had cleaners come through this morning and clean up the mess, all the new furniture will be delivered tomorrow while we are both at school. I leave her in the entryway as I head for my office to get ahead on the workload, we're having issues with the CHU board wanting to push us out. The fuckers were happy to accept our money but hate that we have a say in anything. Crue and Saint are doing their best to keep things on track there but I know it's hard on them. Beck is killing it in Alaska and has even started taking over managing the chains of resorts. Darius is even excelling in the operations department in Chicago. I drop into my seat and wake my computer, not a second later a Zoom call pops up.

I hit answer, sit back in my seat as Crue and Saint's faces fill the screen. "Fuck me, it's like Halloween came early looking at your face." I flip Saint off just Darius and Beck join the call. Beck looks like he's just woken up and Darius looks like he's just finished working out.

"What's up, fuckers?" D says in greeting.

"My cock was until I saw your face," Crue snarks, earning

a glare from D, and we all laugh. It feels good laughing with my brothers again, it's been a minute.

"Fuck you, dipshit! What do you fuckers want, I got shit to do today," Darius barks out.

"What shit?" I ask. D rubs the back of his neck and darts his gaze away for a second. "Darius?" I push.

"Fuck, okay. Leah is busting her ass to finish her classes online and wants to head back to CHU after Easter break. She says she can't be away from Katie anymore. It's not like I can say no."

I pin him with a dry stare. "Yeah, you can, just say N.O." I spell it out for the dumbass.

"Dude, your sister is just as stubborn as you and will withhold—"

"Moving on!" Beck shouts, cutting in so Darius doesn't finish that cringe-worthy sentence. "Look, I have something to say as well." I focus on Beck and can see the unease written across his face. "I know we all agreed to head to the cabin for Easter, it will be our first real holiday with Dawson as a family, because I sure as fuck am not counting last Christmas but—" Beck shifts his gaze to me and I know what he is going to say. "Val's coming with me and if you don't like it, fuck you." The others remain silent as they wait for me to speak. I see it in Beck's eyes that he won't budge on this and I respect that.

"Okay." The four of them all look shocked as fuck at my answer.

"Seriously?" Crue asks.

"Yes, dumb ass, we all need to be there and Leah text me telling me that Nathan is coming with you lot anyway." Saint and Crue nod.

"Yeah, he's been kicking it with Katie a lot lately, so she and Leah invited him." I nod my agreement.

"How is Katie holding up?" Beck asks. Saint and Crue's

faces both morph into a weird as fuck look that I can't decipher.

"She's uh… Getting there," Saint says.

"Speaking of bringing extras—" I glare at Darius through the screen in warning, the fucker just smirks at me. "Corvin is bringing a plus one, aren't ya, buddy?" If looks could kill, Darius would be six feet in a hole right now.

"What the fuck?"

"Who?"

"Leah's gonna kill you," Beck, Saint and Crue all say in unison. I pinch the bridge of my nose and lean back in my seat praying for calm, but when my four best friends are involved nothing is ever stress free.

"Corvin?" Beck snaps. I focus back on the screen and decide to just tell them the truth.

"Alexa Sutton will be coming with me." Beck, Crue and Saint frown for a beat until Beck clicks.

"Cody's sister?" he breathes out.

"Yes," I grit out.

"Why the fuck is she meeting us there?" Saint asks.

"Oh, she isn't meeting us there, she'll be flying in with dear old Corv, it makes sense they should fly together since she is living with him." I'm going to fucking kill Darius when I see the smug prick.

"What the fuck!"

"Dude!"

"Are you out of your fucking mind?" The three of them say at once. I ignore their questions.

"None of you get a say in this shit. She's staying with me for a while longer until she moves into her dorm room. I don't want to hear a fucking word about it from any of you—."

Crus cuts me off before I can finish. "Katie told us she's seventeen. What the fuck are you doing with a minor, Corvin?" I scrub a hand down my face in frustration, I don't need his shit today and I sure as fuck don't need their judgment.

"She isn't fifteen, dumbass, she is legal to consent," I growl, getting fucking annoyed now. "Keep your noses out of my shit. I don't need you guys lecturing me. I know it's fucked up and wrong but…" I have no idea how to voice what the fuck is happening between me and Alexa.

"You don't need to say anything," Becks says. "I may be wrong but this is the first time you've answered a group call since you left so she has my vote." I frown.

"Vote for what?" I ask.

"Clearly whatever she is doing is helping bring you out of the pits of despair. The fact she is Cody's sister is weird is fuck but who are we all to judge. I mean, your best friend is fucking your little sister." Crue and Saint burst out laughing while Darius fires off at Beck. I'll admit that stupid ass comment has me smiling. I spend the next hour filling them on what shit Alexa has pulled and yes, they all fucking laughed their asses off. We end the call after managing to talk about business for a minute. I dig into my workload, I'm on a roll and smashing through all of it when a knock on the door draws my attention. I look up to see Alexa standing there awkwardly.

"You okay?" I ask, a whoosh of air escapes her and her shoulders deflate. I climb to my feet, round the desk and don't stop until I'm standing in front of her. "Jail bait?" I push.

She slowly lifts her gaze back to mine before she speaks. "Some lady just dropped off bags of clothes. I told her I'd come to get you but she said not to worry because they're all for me. I never asked you to buy me shit, Corvin. I'm not your charity case!" I knew she would be pissed about this.

"If you don't like them, sell them, give them to charity because I don't give a fuck. You have a backpack with clothes in it, jail bait. You needed new shit so I got it for you. No strings attached, okay? Your books will be delivered today as well."

"Stop." I clamp my mouth closed. "Stop doing all of this shit for me! I don't need you to do any of it, I don't want any of it."

"Then fucking dump it! I don't care what the fuck you do with it. I did it to help you not piss you off. I have to head to practice. Come, stay or do whatever you want," I say as I brush past her and head upstairs to change.

Travis pushed me fucking hard today and I needed it. I was too caught up in my own head and needed to focus on something else. I half expect to walk outside and find my car gone but low and behold, there it is unscathed without a scratch on it. The whole drive home I'm a ball of nerves, I'm worried that she has either burnt the building down or done something fucking crazy. You never fucking know when it comes to Alexa.

Pulling into the underground garage I debate if I should stay in the car or just get this shit over with and see what damage she has caused now.

"Fuck it," I grit out as I climb out of the car and head for the elevator. The whole way up, I keep shifting from foot to foot anxiously. When the elevator announces we're on my floor, I slam my eyes closed and take a breath before slowly opening them and stepping out cautiously. I feel like a kid playing army men the way I stick to the wall and peek around each corner like someone is about to jump out and fight me or some shit. An aroma that has my mouth watering greets me as I slowly slink around the corner into the kitchen. I poke my head around the side and my mouth drops open in shock at the sight. I trip over my own feet and catch myself on the edge of the counter. Alexa turns away from the stove and shoots me a questioning look.

"You look constipated," she deadpans.

I shake my head and stand up straight as I look around the kitchen. She's cooked and it smells divine, but I'm also scared shitless that she has poisoned the food or worse, done a Leah and put laxatives in it. I climb onto one of the stools and watch her as she goes about her business. I'm twenty and have no fucking idea how to cook shit without burning it, so the fact a seventeen-year-old is in my kitchen and cooking a gourmet fucking meal has me feeling slightly inadequate.

She flips one of the steaks in the pan and peers at me over her shoulder and asks, "How was practice, darling?" I can't contain the laughter that bubbles out of me. She shoots me a smile and a wink as she goes back to her task.

Once I manage to get my laughter under control, I answer her, "Fucking hard. I needed it though." She nods her head as she begins to remove pans from the elements and starts plating the food. Fuck me, she's made steak, greens, mashed potatoes, pumpkin and some other shit that smells scrumptious and has my mouth watering. She rounds the counter and places the plate in front of me and claims the stool beside me with her plate in front of her. Everything looks amazing but still, I don't touch a single thing.

"Dig in." I side eye her and watch as she digs into her meal, fuck this. I reach out and snag her plate ignoring her protests and switch it with mine. "What the hell, Reaper?"

I pin her with a dry stare. "Seriously? After all the shit you've pulled you really think I trust you enough to eat something you've made and not think it's laced with something?" She scrunched her face in thought for a second before shrugging her shoulders and nodding.

"Fair enough." Why the fuck does that answer not put me at ease? I watch her out of the corner of my eye start to eat again and decide to take the risk of trying it. I mean, if I die, at least I know she'll be stuck in here with my rotting corpse—I made sure not to give her the pin to the elevator. I moan at the taste of the food. She's a fucking amazing cook and holy shit, I've never tasted a steak that can melt in your mouth like this one.

"This is fucking amazing!" I say around a mouthful of food. She smirks cockily and raises a brow. "Who taught you how to cook?"

"YouTube." I frown, she takes pity on me and elaborates. "My parents never gave a shit about me, Reaper. I'm the disappointment of my family, so I didn't get the help from them that my sisters did. I mean shit, we bury Cody, then they're on the next flight to Thailand without a word. I only found out because Keeley posted a picture online with the caption *'Time to heal as a family.'*" She shrugs it off like it doesn't bother her, but I see it in the way her shoulders hunch that them not including her hurts.

"Cody was the one who would look out for you, wasn't she?" She glares down at her plate and nods stiffly.

"She was the only person who gave a fuck about me," she whispers brokenly, and guilt swarms inside me.

CHAPTER ELEVEN

I know I have a part to play in order for my new plan to work but it's fucking hard when I blame him for the loss of my sister. I still have no idea why the fuck he is putting up with the shit I have put him through. I've cost him hundreds of thousands of dollars' worth of damage and he's just paid my education. I school my features and make sure to keep the emotion out of my voice as I divulge information I know will go a long way in him trusting me and letting me in.

"Cody was the one I called the first time Jason hit me." I see him stiffen, then white knuckles his knife and fork, out of the corner of my eye but he remains silent, waiting for me to continue. "I was a foolish idiot thinking it was a one-time thing, I knew he was dabbling in drugs but I ignored it because for the first time in my life I had someone." I sigh and push my food around my plate.

"Why did you leave?" he asks quietly.

"It took a minute, I met Jason at my high school when I was sixteen. I was dumb and fell for the first guy who uttered those three stupid little words. I never loved him. I wanted to but I just couldn't. For the first few months everything was great but then his parents pushed him to get straight A's so he would pop pills to stay up later studying. He was snappy and angry on those days but never laid a hand on me until one of his friends gave him a bag of coke, then shit went south when he was coming down. The first time he hit me, I called Cody and she got me out but three days later I caved and answered his call, He swore he was sorry and told me he missed me. I couldn't hide out in her dorm forever, so I went back."

"How long did it carry on?" The anger in his tone is clear. I lock my own emotions down and force myself to finish the story.

"Another four or so months, it wasn't long after I graduated but the last time was the worst. He cracked my ribs and did damage to my face. Cody got me out and I never went back. I stayed with her for a while but I knew me being at CHU was keeping her from hanging out with you and her friends so I lied. I told her Mom and Dad called and wanted me to go home. I could see the relief on her face and I couldn't blame her. She was in love and living her best life. I didn't want to hold her back any more than I already was."

"Where did you go?"

"I couch surfed on friend's couches or stayed in abandoned houses. I didn't have the luxury of money coming out of my ass, so hotels were out of the question." I force a laugh but he doesn't join me.

"How did you get out here, Alexa?"

"I stole Cody's debit card and used the last bit of cash I had. My parents found out I stole it and canceled it."

"And they never questioned why you were out here?" I turn to him and pin him with a dumbfounded look.

"They hopped on a fucking plane to Thailand without me. Do you really think they give a fuck about where I am?" I hear the bitterness that coats my own words. We both remain silent for a moment lost in our own thoughts until he breaks it.

"I'm sorry I took her away from you. I had no idea you were with her at CHU."

"It's not your fault," I mutter.

"You'll never have to worry about money again, Alexa." I frown at him. "Scream, shout, curse me out or whatever you want but I have set up a bank account for you with two-hundred grand in it." My mouth drops open. "Use it how you please and if you need more just call me. I want you to not have to worry about working while you're at school and just focus on your studies. I'm hoping that money will ease some of the stress for you."

"What the fuck? You can't just throw money around like that!" I shout at him.

"Why not? It's my fucking money and I can do what I want with it. I don't care, jail bait, spend it or don't, but it's in an account under your name and only you can touch it."

"This is fucking crazy."

"No, what's crazy is you still answering that piece of shit's fucking calls after what he did to you!" His words leak with venom as his eyes drill into me, holding me captive, the look in his eyes is one of protectiveness.

"You don't get to sit there on your high horse and judge me," I force out through clenched teeth. "You know nothing about me and yet you think you have the right to judge me because I told you a sob story?" I scoff for added effect. "I don't need your fucking pity. I'm not a victim of anything. I'm a fucking survivor and choose not to dwell on the past that I allowed myself to live." Truth is, I'm not really angry at him, I'm pissed at myself for putting up with Jason's shit as long as I did.

"I don't pity you. I fucking admire you for not giving up and fighting for what you want even though you've been dealt a shit fucking hand in life." I'm rendered speechless. I have no idea what to say to that, not even Cody would acknowledge that aloud. "Don't let that piece of shit make you feel like you owe him something. You have a chance at a fresh start and building a better life for yourself, don't squander it."

I'm stuck sleeping in Corvin's bed for another night until the new furniture arrives tomorrow. I lay here staring up at the ceiling still reeling from our conversation at dinner. How can you hate someone so much and yet feel a connection with them that you have never felt with anyone else? I roll over and try to force myself to sleep before Corvin comes to bed, but I can't stop overthinking to achieve that. My phone rings, pulling me from my inner turmoil—Corvin gave it back after dinner. I reach over and grab it from the bedside table and groan when I see Katie's name.

I answer the call and bring the phone to my ear. "What do you want Katie?"

"Just to see if you're okay." The watery tone of her voice tells me she's been crying.

"I'm fine." When she doesn't reply straight away I ask, "Are you okay?"

A watery chuckle escapes her. "No. I'm not okay but what's new."

I'm not heartless enough to end the call so I ask. "What happened?"

"You don't need to hear my shit, Lexi."

"Distract me from my own drama… please."

It takes her a second but she caves and talks. "I recently found out I was pregnant."

My stomach sinks. "You said *was*." A sob escapes her, I remain silent waiting for her to gather herself.

"I found out the week Cody… left. She was the only person I told. I had planned to tell the guys but then everything happened and I lost the baby." Guilt washes over me, she called me the other day and I was a bitch to her. I've got a first class ticket to hell for being such a cunt to her when she was dealing with this loss.

"I'm so sorry, Katie." I mean it, I am sorry because no one deserves to lose a child.

"I was happy, ya know. I wanted the baby, I know Saint and Crue don't want kids and I would have raised it on my own without an argument. I never knew I wanted to be a mom until the option was ripped away from me."

"Did… did you tell them?" She sniffs and when she doesn't answer straightaway, I have my answer. "They found out, didn't they?"

"Yeah, they came over and found the test." She breaks down and I feel like an asshole. I'm sure that if Cody was here she would be there for her friend. I may hate Corvin but that doesn't mean I have to project that hate onto anyone else.

"I'm so sorry, Katie. I wish there was something I could do," I say honestly, meaning every word.

"Just promise you're coming to the cabin for Easter so I can hug you." A whoosh of air escapes me. Corvin told me about this trip and I really don't want to go anywhere with him, but I also know if I do this it will bring me closer to reaching my goal.

"Yeah, I'll be there."

"Thank you, Lexi."

"Uh, for what?" I asked, confused why she would be thanking me right now.

"For distracting me from… what happened." Sadness laces each of her words. "I'm just a mess right now."

"You have every right to be a mess." She sniffles again and my heart aches for her.

"They're so angry with me, Lexi. I fucked up so bad and now I'm scared I'll lose them." I'm not qualified to be giving any one relationship advice right now. I mean, I'm fucking my sisters ex.

"If they can't understand why you didn't tell them straight away, then make them understand, Katie. Life is too fucking short for *what ifs*."

"They won't even return my calls. I went to their dorm and they wouldn't let me in. They have never raised their voices at me before, but I didn't even recognize them. I know this is a lot for them as well but I just…"

"Needed them to hold you through the pain," I whisper, knowing exactly what she means. Katie and I talked for a while longer until her friend Nathan showed up at her dorm. We ended the call with me promising to call her tomorrow and let her know how my first day went at WFU. I'll admit, I got a wee bit choked up when she told me she was proud of me for doing this and not rejecting Corvin's offer.

Nerves thrum through me as Corvin and I walk side-by-side out of the administration building after getting our class schedules. Students mill about the busy halls. Some guy runs past and knocks into me, sending me staggering, Corvin wraps his arm around my waist and draws me into his side while shooting a glare at the guy.

"Watch it," he snarls, the poor nerdy looking guy pales and nods before dashing away. "You gonna be okay to find your way? I have to go meet the coach." I look up at him and nod.

"Yeah, I'll figure it out." He pursues his lips to the side studying me for a moment before he reluctantly nods.

"If you need me just text or call and I'll be here." I feel like there is a double meaning to his words but he doesn't elaborate further. We stand here awkwardly, just staring at each other for a while until he leans down, places a kiss on my cheek and whispers in my ear, "You got this, jail bait. If you can fuck with me and wreck my house and car, you can handle college." Laughter burst out of me without consent. He pulls back, shoots me a wink and stalks out of the doors to go meet with his new coach. I should feel relieved that he's gone and left me to do my own thing but… I don't.

I feel like I can conquer this shit with him by my side, and now without him I feel lost. I shake my head and push those thoughts away. I cannot get attached or allow myself to feel anything but hatred for Corvin Williams, no matter how nice he tries to be or how kind he shows himself to be. I need to remain strong and make sure my sister gets her revenge on the man that broke her.

CHAPTER TWELVE

Corvin

I hate leaving her on her own but I know me hovering will just make her angry and I'm not trying to pick a fight with her when we all know the girl hits harder than most of the guys on the team. She proved that when she trashed my house and car. I'll admit, the closer I get toward the gym I grow a bit nervous. I know WFU's coach is only new and been here about six months but he's the coach that has brought this team to where they are. They were good before but they could be great now and have a chance at the championship.

I push through the gymnasium doors and follow the signs to the locker rooms where I know the coach's office will be near, they always are. I stop outside the closed door with the name badge *Coach Barkley*. I wipe my clammy hands on my jeans and pull myself together, I never thought I would ever join a team that wasn't my own. CHU is my home and that team will always be my heart team but right now I can't be anywhere near there and this is the only choice I have if I want to go pro. I need to do this and Travis said this school will help me get there.

I knock twice and wait. "Come in," someone shouts. I

square my shoulders as I push the door open and immediately freeze in the entryway.

"What the fuck," I breathe out, sitting there behind the wooden desk with a shit eating grin on his face is none other than my trainer Travis, and standing beside him is the asshole I saw talking to Alexa when we were here yesterday.

"Come on in, my man, and have a seat." I step into the office and close the door behind me, but I don't take a seat like Travis instructed, opting to stand instead. Travis just smiles and shakes his head as he leans back in his seat. "Corvin meet Ash, he is WFU's starting QB but as you know due to him needing shoulder surgery he is unable to play out the rest of the season." I size the fucker up and he does the same to me.

"Nice to meet you," he says. I meet his gaze but say nothing. After yesterday and the way he was with my girl—-wait, what the fuck? No, Alexa isn't my girl and can do whatever the fuck she wants!

"Corvin?" I blink a couple times to focus and look back to Travis. "I know this must be a surprise for you."

I snort. "Gee, what gave the surprise away?" I snark.

"Don't be a dick," Trav snaps.

"You lied to me!" I snarl.

"The fuck I did. You never asked what I did for a living, you assumed all I did was train you and a couple of others. That isn't on me, that's on you. I mean for fuck's sake, Corvin, what school do you know would take on a new QB halfway through the season without seeing him play?" I grit my teeth knowing he's right, I did find it fucking odd. "You're here because I've seen what you can do and I know you can help get us to the championship but you'll be training harder than the rest of the team. I've seen your game tapes."

I scowl at him. "What the fuck is that supposed to mean?" I growl.

"It means, I know you're used to the halfback and wide

receiver from CHU as well as your running back and tight end but you won't have your friends here. You'll need to rely on your new teammates and put in the work to gel with them. You'll be here at six every morning and each day after classes. You'll be here again till six or when I say you're done. I won't go easy on you. I told you before that you could be great and I meant that."

I step further into the room and cut my gaze to Ash who doesn't seem pissed about me brushing him off. "You good with just handing over your position, just like that?" I say while clicking my fingers together.

He exhales and nods. "I won't lie. No, I'm not thrilled about it and honestly, I fucking hate that I'm not the one leading my team to the state championships. But at the end of the day, this is what's best for the team and coach says you're the best." I look back to Travis who nods his head confirming what Ash says.

"If I do this, I choose the plays against CHU." Travis opens his mouth to protest but I push on. "I know my boys. Saint and Crue won't go easy on the team because of me, if anything they will go harder to prove a point that I should have stayed at CHU. I know that team and I know their plays better than anyone." Ash and Travis exchange a loaded look before Trav looks back to me and nods stiffly, clearly not liking my terms.

"I've cleared it with the staff on campus. You need to keep an average of A's in your core classes and nothing lower than a C+ in your other classes. I know you want to go pro and be drafted, but if that doesn't pan out you need something to fall back on." I chuckle and shake my head.

"You clearly didn't research me enough if you think I care about failing school." Travis frowns. "I own BCD'S with my four best friends. We dominate the stock market and own hotels and resorts all over the world and pretty soon we are about to acquire a tech company. Trust me when I tell you,

I'm not worried about failing or worrying about making enough money."

"Money won't get you in the NFL," Ash adds, earning a glare from me.

"No, it won't. But hard work and determination will, and I have both of things, Ashley." He narrows his eyes at me which brings a smile to my own face.

"Cut the shit, Corvin. Go you for being young and rich but that doesn't mean you're exempt from training and by my clock, you're already late for practice so get your ass changed. You owe me a hundred burpees and ten laps of the field." I bite my tongue to keep from snapping at my new coach. If he thinks he's going to scare me off, he has another thing coming. I need to do this to prove to myself and the others that I'm not a fuck up and I can get my shit together. Losing Cody has rocked the foundations of my life but I can't let it hold me back any longer. I need to do this and start the healing process. I have to so I can be there for Alexa when she breaks because I know it's coming. Her little compliant act isn't fooling me, I know she has a trump card up her sleeve that is going to sting worse than getting sacked.

The moment Travis tells me to hit the showers I could fucking cry. The prick kept his word and pushed me harder than the rest of the team. The team isn't happy with bringing in a new QB instead of using the backup, but the truth is, the kid's throwing arm is shit and he couldn't throw a fucking Hail Mary if it hit him in the dick. The team says nothing to me as we enter the locker room and honestly, I don't give a fuck. I'm here to play the game and that's it. I make quick work of showering and changing so I can get my ass across campus and meet up with Alexa and find out how her morning went. At least with me training late I know I won't have to come back and pick her up. She finishes her community service at six every day, so it works out for the both of us.

The moment I exit the gym, I slam to a stop and glare at the back of Ash's head. The fucker stands there talking to Alexa, who has a smile on her face. This smile isn't like the ones she gives me, this one is unfiltered and not forced, easy and freely given. I climb down the stairs drawing both their attention to me. The smile vanishes from her face as she looks at me.

"What are you doing here?" I snap. A look of hurt flashes in her eyes before she quickly masks it.

"Coming to see you, jackass, but you can choke on a dick now," she grits out before turning and rushing back toward the main building.

"Fuck!" I snap.

"Bit harsh, don't ya think?" I snap my gaze to Ash, shooting him a warning look.

"Stay the fuck away from Alexa." The prick quirks a brow challenging me.

"Why? She made it clear a minute ago that you're not her boyfriend, so that means she's free game, right?" I step into Ash until we are chest to chest. I'm a couple inches taller than him so I make sure to use that to my advantage as I look down at him.

"You so much as touch a single hair on her head and I'll make sure you never throw another fucking ball again, feel me?" I don't wait for an answer as I shoulder past him and chase after Alexa. My long legs eat up the space she's put between us. I reach out and grip her hand, pulling her to a stop. She spins on me and yanks her hand free.

"Fuck. You," she snarls.

I smirk. "Right now?"

She scrunches her face in confusion. "What?"

"You said *fuck you* and I asked if you meant you'd do it

right now, because I'm down." She stomps her foot and huffs out her annoyance.

"You're such a dick and I can't wait to move out!" Fuck, that hurt.

"I'm sorry," I blurt out, shocking the both of us.

"Uh, for what?"

I shrug my shoulders suddenly feeling vulnerable. "For snapping at you, you can come see me anytime you want."

She throws her hands in the air. "Then why were you a dick?"

I decide to be honest. "It pissed me off seeing you talk to another guy."

Her brows raise to her hairline, surprised by my confession. "Reaper, you're not my boyfriend, fuck, you're not even my friend. Who I talk to or fuck isn't—" Before she can finish that fucking ridiculous sentence, I snake my hand out, grip the back of her neck and pull her forward until she is pressed against me.

"You think for a second that I am going to let anyone else touch you, then you're out your fucking mind, jail bait. No one is fucking you but *me*!"

"Pretty territorial for someone with commitment issues, don't ya think?"

Her words are like a bucket of ice water being doused over me. I release her and step back. "You're right. I do have commitment issues but if you knew why then you would understand. Enjoy the rest of your day. I'll see you at the car after practice," I say before walking away from her, without a single glance back.

I fucking hate that she can push me and force my hand. I need to keep my head clear and focus on my goal which is to go pro. Alexa Sutton is a distraction I can't afford. Darius and my sister flying out this weekend couldn't come soon enough. I need someone who is on my side and I hope with them being here it will help Alexa see I'm not a fucking bad guy. I never meant for Cody to die but each day I'm learning that what happened to her was out of my control. Did I love her? Yes. But I also know I can't stop living my life because she died. Leah was right, Cody wouldn't want me wasting my life. Alexa is right, she does need to move out because I'm starting to blur the lines between just fucking and wanting more for the first time ever.

But why does the idea of her moving out and going home to an empty penthouse every night fill me with sadness? Fuck, am I falling for the jail bait?

CHAPTER THIRTEEN

Alexa

The rest of the day passes by at a freaking snail's pace. I get side glances from the girls and the guys make it no secret that they are checking me out. Lunch was spent outside under a tree by myself. I even text Katie to tell her how my day was going, and she added Leah and Val to the chat. Unlike Corvin, I don't blame Beckett's girlfriend for my sister's death. She actually seems nice. Leah and her both say they are excited to meet me. They also told me that they all plan to fly out here for Corvin's first game back and asked me to keep it a secret. It feels weird talking to them and being friendly, when I have plans to ruin Corvin.

I check the time on my phone and see I only have twenty minutes before I'm finished my first day of community service. I decide to quit sweeping the workshop and look around to find it empty. Yes! I drop the broom and make my way over to the Excalibur, which is on a Mustang's body. A project car that the class is working on. It reminds me of Cruella Deville's car but it's stunning. Its V8 engine sits on a block beside it, and the interior is a plush white leather with the original dash still intact and polished perfectly. It's a convertible, this car isn't like any of the ones you see these days, no electronics or computer, the roof doesn't have a button to push to close it for you, it's all done manually. I run my hand down the side of the door and smile. I would love to build something like this. I would love to just restore an old school car back to its former glory and stare at it knowing that I was the one who did that.

The hood folds up on either side and I peek inside to see that they have already started to assemble things. I make my way over to the engine and see that the timing chain and the cam tower are leaking oil. I shake my head and grab a ten-mil wrench and reach in to start tightening the timing chain.

"You shouldn't be doing that," I scream and drop the wrench. It clangs against the ground as I turn to find a middle-age man standing in the doorway, with blue overalls on that are covered in oil and other stains. I remain silent as he slowly makes his way over to me, grabs the wrench off the ground and looks over the engine frowning. "What were you doing?"

I shuffle awkwardly from foot to foot as I answer him. "The timing chain is loose and I was tightening it, the cam tower is also leaking oil." He snaps his gaze at me and frowns.

"I told those idiots not to put the oil in until after the engine was fitted," he says, clearly exasperated.

"Sorry, I'll be on my way now," I say as I turn to leave and hope to God I didn't just fuck up my chances of getting into this class.

"Wait." I freeze mid step and slowly turn back to face the man. "Who are you?"

"Uh, I just started today and have to clean the workshops every day—"

"You're the community service kid who is trying to get into my shop class?" I cringe and nod stiffly.

"Yep." He looks me over not in a sexual way but in a way that shows me he's trying to figure me out.

"How did you know about this?" he asks, motioning to the engine.

I shrug my shoulders. "Cars are kind of my thing."

He nods. "Tell ya what, kid, I've been trying to get these knuckleheads to figure out that the chain was loose for a couple weeks and they couldn't. If you fix this and explain to me what parts you are fixing and talk me through what's wrong with it, I'll make sure Barkley transfers you to my class as your community service time instead of cleaning every day."

My eyes widen. "Seriously?"

He smiles kindly. "Yeah."

"Why would you help me?" I ask skeptically.

He takes a deep breath before answering. "I've been where you are and I want to give you the same opportunity I was afforded." That shocks the shit out of me. I nod my head and quickly race around the room grabbing the tools I need before going to work on the engine. As I get to work to fix the problems, he introduces himself and he and I talk as I start fixing the chain. He's actually a really cool guy and knows a fuck load about cars. He tells me the seven guys in his class are shit at rebuilds and only want to work on Japanese imports. One of them was even dumb enough to suggest trying to put a wastegate in this classic project.

"What the hell?" I say with a laugh.

Shannon laughs and nods. "I joke you not. I wanted to slap him upside the head." We both laugh at the stupidity of some people. Our laughter cuts off when the door opens to reveal an angry-looking Corvin. My eyes widen at the sight of him before I look to the clock on the wall and curse when I see the time. It's nearly seven and I told him I would meet him at six. "Can I help you?" Shannon asks. Corvin doesn't acknowledge him or even look toward him, just keeps his gaze on me. Rather than making a scene, I quickly put the tools down and step around Shannon heading for Corvin but stop a couple feet away to turn back.

"Thank you, I'm sorry for keeping you so late..." Regret blooms inside me, I never finished the task he set for me. "Thank you for the chance—"

Shannon cuts me off before I can finish. "Leave Barkley to me. I'll see you first thing tomorrow morning." My eyes widen in surprise.

"Really?" I can hear the hope in my own voice.

"Yeah, kid. You're good and picked up a lot of shit I didn't see. I'll have your new class schedule waiting for you on my desk tomorrow."

I beam at him before racing across the room and flinging myself at him. I wrap my arms around his neck, hugging. He tenses for a second before gently pushing me back and shooting a disapproving look that lacks heat. Oh fuck! Realization dawns on me and I want the floor to open up and swallow me whole when I realize I just hugged my teacher!

I blanch up at him. "I'm so sorry, I'm gonna go now before I do something else." He laughs and I mentally facepalm myself. I turn and rush toward Corvin, he steps out of the way. I grab his hand and practically drag him from the building, needing to get the hell out of there so I can die of shame privately. The moment we step outside, Corvin rips his hand from mine and storms off toward the car, clearly pissed off. I roll my eyes and follow after him. I'm not going to let his sour mood dampen mine, because I'm on cloud fucking nine right now!

We both slip into the car and immediately the tension amps up—it's so thick. I see how stiff he is out of the corner of my eye and I begin to wonder what the hell happened at practice for him to be this wound up. I'm about to ask him what's wrong, but then I remember that I don't care and it's not my problem if he's having a bad day. The ride home is tense and not a word is spoken the whole way. Even as we ride the elevator up to the penthouse, he says nothing and his mood is starting to fucking piss me off. The doors open and he practically runs to get away from me. I glare at his back refusing to comment. He goes straight upstairs, rolling my eyes I head for my room. I flick the lights on and gasp. All the new furniture litters the room, the bed even has new covers. I rush into the closet to see that the hordes of clothes he bought me have all now been hung up.

I go into the bathroom next and try the shower but no water comes out, I frown as a thought hits me. He has all the money in the world, pays for my school and dorm, gets me new clothes and new bedroom shit but can't fix a shower?

"That motherfucker!" I grit out. He isn't fixing the shower on purpose, so I have no choice but to share his. Oh, you sneaky little bitch. You are going to pay for that, asshole. I decide to devise a plan to fuck with him one last time before I move out. A smile spreads across my face when an idea hits me. Oh, Reaper, you should never have given me the code for the elevator, now you are going to pay.

Corvin hasn't spoken a word to me for nearly two days. It's Friday and the vibe around campus is infectious as students make plans for their weekend. I hate that his silent treatment is bothering me when it shouldn't. I hate him. I keep repeating that in my head as I walk around and hand out the flyers I printed this morning in the library. Random students rush over to grab a copy and I smile as I hand them all one telling them to spread the word. Part of me felt bad for thinking of doing this to him, then this morning when I woke up, I made a deal with myself. If he spoke to me then I would veto this idea but he didn't, and now he will pay the price for this.

Once all the flyers have been handed out I make my way

to Shannon's class. True to his word, he managed to get Moss to change his mind. I have no idea how he did it and I didn't question him, I'm just fucking grateful to be in his class and not have to do community service every fucking day. I'm also not stupid enough to think Corvin and his lawyer didn't have a helping hand in this. Just as I enter the building and reach my class, my phone vibrates. I pull it out and roll my eyes at the sight of Jason's name. I'll never tell him or admit it, but I took Corvin's advice and stopped replying to Jason's texts and answering his calls. I fucking hate to admit it but he wasn't wrong when he said Jason would never change. After the first day of ignoring him, the abusive voicemails and text messages started flooding in. I don't even open the messages I just delete them all now.

My phone begins to ring and I'm about to hit ignore thinking it's Jason but when I see *Reaper* appear on the screen, I answer it. "What do you want, Reaper?" I snap, annoyed as fuck that he won't speak to me but thinks calling is okay?

"I'll be late home tonight, got some shit to do after practice. I got you an Uber for after school." I grit my teeth in annoyance, for the past two days I've had to wait for him to finish practice before going home. It's not like I have a car to get home or money to pay for a cab.

"Cool, anything else?" I grit out.

"Yeah, there will be an envelope on the counter for you when you get home." I tense.

"What is it?" Skepticism is clear in my tone.

"The keys to your dorm room, you move in on Monday. There is also a debit card in there for you as well. Got to go, jail bait." He ends the call, not giving me a chance to say anything back. I mean really, what the fuck could I have said? I stand here for a minute reeling, he kept his word and really did get me my own dorm room and a bank account. I thought he was talking out his ass, honestly. I mean, no one does this shit for free. Ever since he came to find me on Tuesday night, he hasn't said a word to me, not even when I walked out of his shower last night trying to get a reaction out of him. He did look me over and I saw the longing in his gaze, but the dead giveaway was the tent in the front of his sweats. I thought for sure he would come to my room last night after my show and fuck me, but he didn't.

Why the fuck does the fact he won't talk to me, or even acknowledge me, bother me so damn much? My eyes widen. Oh, fuck no. Nope, I'm not even going to think that because fuck that. After the surprise I have planned for him tonight, he will hate me and then I'll be back on track and make sure the line between us doesn't get blurred again—well, for me anyway.

CHAPTER FOURTEEN

Corvin

Making my way out to my car, I find myself smiling. I'm actually excited to see my sister and Darius and think it will be good having them here to break the tension between me and Alexa. After the revelation I came to the other day, I've made sure to keep my distance and my dick in my pants. I know my silent treatment is getting to her, and after her little fucking show last night I nearly caved. I had to talk myself out of marching my ass downstairs to her room and fucking her until we both blacked out. I managed to stop myself and I'm man enough to admit I jerked off to memories of her naked and riding me in the hallway.

Fuck, for the past few days I have tried to keep my distance, not speak to her or even be in the same room as her for more than five minutes, with the exclusion of the ride to and from school. That shit is pure fucking torture! Being that close to her where I can brush against her arm, smell her shampoo and just fucking breathe her in is pure fucking hell. I know I'm fucked up. This whole situation is fucked up. Thing is, I know I should feel guilty for all of this and at the start I did, but now, I crave her. She hasn't done anything or gone out of her way to make me feel anything other than disdain, but what she doesn't know is her mere presence and constant snarky remarks are helping me heal and push forward from the loss we have both suffered.

I had to switch my car out at lunch today and pick up the new Range Rover I just bought so I would have enough seats to pick Leah and Darius up. The whole way to the airport I can't keep the smile off my face. I'm looking forward to Alexa finally being able to meet Leah. She thinks I have no idea that she has been messaging my sister and the others, but Leah told me. I'm glad that she has been talking to them. I know she doesn't have any friends, if she did she would have called them to bail her crazy ass out of jail and not me.

"I'm so glad we could surprise you," Leah says from her seat beside me. I shake my head and shoot her a smile. She isn't wrong, they got me fucking good I'll give them that. Not only did Darius and Leah fly out, Crue, Saint and Beck came as well. I was fucking blown away when I pulled up to the pick-up lane and saw the five of them standing there. Thank fuck I got a car with seven seats or two of them would be catching an Uber.

"You all got me good, ya fuckers," I say while looking at my boys in the rearview mirror.

"Bitch, please, no way were we letting Darius fly out here and get a front-row seat to experience the cray cray you live with without us." Rolling my eyes I shoot Saint a glare in the mirror which just causes him to laugh.

"Stop it. Lexi is cool and I'm excited to finally meet her," Leah says. I shoot her a grateful smile for her support of Alexa.

"Goldie, you love everyone, so your vote doesn't count." My sister peers around her seat to glare at her boyfriend.

"Explains why I like you then, huh?" Everyone bursts out

laughing, we all know that remark is going to piss Darius off. The guy is so overdramatic when it comes to my sister.

"Say that shit again, I dare you," D taunts.

Leah smiles wickedly. "Babe, you left yourself wide open for that one. But I don't just like you, I love you." I make a gagging sound, earning a laugh from Beck and the duo in back.

"Damn fucking right you do, Now, tell Becky you don't love him." Beckett snorts and shoves Darius in the arm.

"Don't bring me into your shit, asshole. I'm just here to make sure that Corvin doesn't get murdered by the underage captive he has locked in his tower." They all laugh at my expense. I grit my teeth and choose not to comment on that remark, or I risk showing my true feelings.

We pull onto my street and I frown at all the cars parked along the sidewalk. I pull into the underground garage, not overthinking it too much. I help carry the bags as we make our way to the elevator. We make small talk on the ride up but everyone falls silent as we near the penthouse as the bass of loud music can be heard through the metal doors. Dread pools inside me. She wouldn't, would she? The moment the doors open I get my answer.

Yes, yes she fucking would.

"Oh fuck," I hear Leah mutter from beside me. Gritting my teeth, I step out of the lift and force my fucking way through the crowd of people I've never fucking seen before. As I look around trying to find the girl who's neck I'm about to fucking wring, I suddenly notice some familiar faces. Vince and Austin raise their beers bottles in greeting. My new fucking team mates are here partying in my fucking house! I look to the left and spot the sound system someone must have brought over just in front of the windows in the living room. I drop the bags in my hands and storm over to it, grip the cord and rip it out of the socket.

The moment the music cuts out, choruses of *what the fuck*

and *who the fuck did that* ring out. I march over to the coffee table in the center of the living room and hop on it. All eyes are on me and that's when I spot the little shit sitting on the counter in the kitchen, directly across from me with a shit eating smile on her face.

"All of you have two fucking minutes to get the fuck out of my house, now!" I roar. The dumb fucks just stand there, looking at me like I've lost my fucking mind. My boys come to stand on either side of the table folding their arms over their chests. "Fucking move!" I yell. They all begin to race toward the elevator. Austin and a couple other guys from the team stop in front of me, I look down my nose at them.

"Sorry, bro, we had no idea this was your spot," Austin says.

"Well, now you do," I snap. I'm being a dick but right now I don't give a fuck. I just need them all gone so I can deal with the little shit that is still smiling at me. I keep my eyes on her the whole fucking time as we wait for every single one of the fuckers to get the fuck out—it takes close to twenty fucking minutes for the last lot to leave. The moment they do, I jump down off the table. Alexa swings around on the counter so her legs dangle over the side facing me. I have to step over bottles, plastic cups and who knows what the fuck else to get to her. The moment I'm within reach she opens her legs wide enough for me to slip in between, we're eye level and I make sure she can see the anger in my gaze.

The dirty little temptress places her hands on top of my shoulders and quirks a brow. "You seem upset, Reaper, want me to rub you better?" she says in the sweetest tone. I grind my teeth so fucking hard my jaw begins to ache.

"Fuck, she really is crazy," I hear Crue say behind me. She doesn't acknowledge him or remove her eyes from mine. I place my hands on the tops of her bare thighs—I know she is only wearing a pair of denim cut-offs and a crop top to fuck with me. Alexa doesn't wear shit like this, she's more of a shirt and jeans type of girl. I feel a shiver roll through her at my touch. A smug sense of satisfaction courses through me, knowing I affect her as much as she does me.

"Jail bait, if you thought throwing a party with all the random fucks you don't even know from school was going to get me to fuck you senseless," her eyes harden and her jaw locks, "you were fucking wrong. If you wanted my attention, you should have said instead of acting like a spoilt little shit who didn't get their favorite toy from Toys'R'Us." She tries to shove me away, but I stand firm and lean forward until my lips ghost over hers, loving the way her pupils dilate. "I told you before, do whatever you want to make yourself feel better but come Monday when you move into your dorm that option is off the table." I pause making sure I have her full attention as I continue. "The moment that option is off the table, you're going to see a side of me that no one else ever has."

Her eyes widen as she flicks her eyes between mine searching for a clue of what I mean. "What side?"

I smirk cockily. "A side that acts like a jealous boyfriend when I have no right to." Her face drops. I expect her to curse me out and promise to maim me, but what I don't expect is for her to slap me across the face. Gasps sound out around the room from the others. I'm too shocked to move or say a thing.

"How fucking dare you!" I hear my sister scream. I hear a scuffle coming from behind but don't look.

"Goldie, stay out of this one, baby. He made his bed now he needs to lay in it." I slowly turn back toward Alexa to see tears in her blue eyes, her bottom lip begins to wobble as she stares at me.

"You don't ever get to say that shit to me!" she screams in my face, tears beginning to leak from her eyes and I'm stunned by the sight of it. "You stand here and act like your fucking commitment issues aren't the reason my sister fucking died, but you think you can call yourself *my* boyfriend?" she scoffs. I never said that, so clearly she misunderstood what I meant, but I don't correct her. "I fucking hate you." I flinch, she sniffs and swipes the tears away but they keep falling. "You know what's worse?" She doesn't give me a chance to answer. "I see it in your eyes, the way you look at me, the way you watch me and my suspicions were confirmed when you saw me with Ash and Shannon." I frown and slowly take a step back. She smiles slyly at me and that's when things click into place.

"You played me," I whisper. She slips off the counter and stands in front of me with her neck craned back so she can meet my gaze.

"You bet your fucking ass I did. This was my *Hail Mary* pass, quarter back, and from the look on your face, I managed to catch you *offside* and score the *touchdown* without you seeing me in your *blindside*." Pain begins to bloom in my chest. "I won the *endgame*."

I stare down at her in a whole new light. I knew she was up to something from the moment she started being nice and called this little truce between us. This, this feeling that I feel right now is the reason I don't commit. Catching feelings for someone gives them power over you and you can never take it back.

"Congratulations, jail bait," I whisper, a small frown marring her face but she quickly schools her features trying to act indifferent. "You managed to succeed in doing what your sister couldn't."

"What's that?" she grits out.

I smile sadly down at her. This is my karma for what I put through Cody through. I deserve this. "You managed to weave your way under my skin and burrow yourself inside me without any fucking effort. You won, Alexa, I give up," I say as I put space between us and raise my hands in surrender. "I hope your revenge was everything you thought it would be. Have a good life, jail bait, you deserve it," I say before turning back to the others. My sister is crying in Darius's hold, while the four guys stand there with malice in their eyes. I shake my head. "I'm gonna head out and get a hotel for the night."

"We're coming with you," Saint says. Crue nods and I smile my thanks as I look to the other three.

Leah has her glare focused on Alexa as she speaks, "Text us the name and room number, we'll meet you there. Alexa and I need to have a little *chat*." Too emotionally spent to argue, I just nod. I don't look back at the girl who managed to burrow herself inside me and force her way into my heart as I leave. Truth is, I think I started developing feelings weeks ago when she would message me every day. Our arguing over text messages became our form of foreplay.

I hate the fact that the girl who died is the one who fought with all she had to get me to love her and I couldn't. Don't get me wrong, I did love Cody, but the way I feel about her sister is so different. Alexa is my oxygen. I became so dependent on her and her daily texts, it was the only way I could get my ass out of bed, knowing I would hear from her in a few hours. She became the anchor I didn't know I needed at the time, but now, she switched to the iceberg that sunk my heart.

CHAPTER FIFTEEN

Alexa

Watching him walking away with his shoulders bunched and his head hung low doesn't fill me with satisfaction or joy from knowing I kept my promise to my sister and broke the guy that destroyed her. When he rounds the corner to the elevator, my legs move on their own accord and I stand at the end of the alcove and watch as the doors open. The three of them step inside with Corvin in the middle. He turns around and the doors begin to close. As he finally lifts his head, our eyes collide and a lump forms in my throat at the sight of the unshed tears in his brown eyes. What breaks me worse than that sight is the sad smile he shoots me, telling me it's okay that I broke him and he doesn't blame me for everything I've done to him. The doors close and I break. I drop to my knees, bury my face in my hands, and cry.

It's not a pretty girl cry. This is the type of crying you do alone in your own room where no one can see you or hear the horrid sounds that come out of your mouth. This pain I feel in my chest is soul deep. The tears aren't just for what I did or how I hurt Corvin, they're for the loss of my best friend and for the shitty hand life dealt me. I've never taken pity on myself like this and allowed myself to cry or feel any type of pity for what I have struggled through since I was a child. Seeing that look of utter devastation and heartache on Corvin's face snapped something inside me, and now I can't stop the tears from falling. I don't even care that I can hear the others speaking in hushed tones behind me. They mean nothing to me and I don't care what they think of me and the mess I currently am.

I flinch away when I feel a hand on my shoulder and snap my tear-stained gaze up to see Leah crouching down beside me with a sad smile on her face. "I get it." I scoff, she has no fucking idea what I'm feeling. "You hurt my brother and I get why, but your sister was my best friend, Alexa. Cody would never have wanted this. Your body isn't a weapon to be used at your disposal, it's your temple to treasure."

I stare at her like she has lost her fucking mind. "You think I slept with your brother for revenge?"

She frowns and cuts a glance at the other before looking back at me. "Isn't that what this is all about?" I push to my feet and try to step around Leah, but she blocks my way. We're the same height, which brings us eye level. They may be siblings but they look nothing alike. Leah's green eyes spark with anger the longer she stares at me, the other two come closer ready to intervene if needed.

"Let me clear a few things up for you, princess. I fucked your brother because I wanted to." Her face scrunches in disgust. "Was my plan to make him fall in love with me?" I don't give her a chance to answer. "Yes, I planned to break him in the same way he broke my sister." Leah growls and steps into me. Beck and Darius rush forward but we ignore them.

"You stupid little girl. Corvin never broke Cody. She was too fucking strong to allow that to happen. Did he hurt her? Yeah, he fucking did and it sucked, but my brother never fucking lied to your sister. Cody knew from the start that he was still fucked up over his ex who fucked his head up and caused my brother to harden his heart to the thought of ever loving someone." I try to mask the confusion from my face but she sees it and pushes on. "Let me tell you something, Alexa, just between us girls, huh?" Her tone is laced with loathing and disgust, and honestly, I can't blame her for hating me. "You won. You got the cold-hearted QB to fall in love with you and you broke him. Well-fucking-done to you. But here's the kicker, my brother never risked anything for your sister, but he fucking risked it all for you and you spat in his face."

"What?" I rasp out confused.

She shakes her head and steps back looking me up and down in disgust. "You're seventeen. He wants to be drafted. If news broke out that he had a seventeen-year-old living with him and was sleeping with her, he would be done. No team would touch him. But, I mean why the fuck would you care? You got your cake and ate it too. Pack your shit and get the fuck out of my brother's house. Enjoy the life he has given you and don't squander it, you ungrateful little shit," she spits at me before shoulder checking me on her way past to the elevators.

"Looks to me Corv wasn't the only one who got their heart broken tonight, huh?" I turn to Darius and scowl at the fucker. "Karma's a real bitch. So glad you got to meet her tonight." He smirks cockily at me before following after his girlfriend. My gaze is drawn to Beckett when he speaks.

"Do yourself a favor, Alexa. Next time you see Corvin, ask him about the voicemail your sister left him. He put up with all the bullshit you put him through because of *her*." My mouth parts and my brows raise in surprise. "Let me tell you something, little girl." His tone is hard and filled with warning. "That man you just hurt is a good fucking guy and one of my best friends. Corvin is the glue that keeps us all together. He would have given you the world and you fucked that all up because you're too self-absorbed to admit you fell in love with the guy you blamed for the loss of your sister. News-flash, kid, he was the fucking one who tried to save her. He never gave up trying to revive her and he is the one who made sure she was treated with dignity and pride up until her funeral. Corvin has never told a single girl he loved them, not even Lana. When Cody lay dying in his arms, he finally said those three fucking words she longed to hear, he did that for *her*." Pain stabs me in the chest. "Take a look in the mirror, kid, because the only bad guy I see around here is you, not Corvin." He turns and walks to the others who hold the doors to the lift open for him.

Just as the doors begin to close Leah darts her arm out and stops them from closing, her gaze bores into mine. "If you come for my brother again, I'll fucking ruin you. But, if the look in your eyes is anything to go by and you do care for Corvin, sort your shit out, Alexa, because none of us will let you near him until you are certain about how you feel." She drops her arm and I stand here stunned silent, watching them disappear inside the metal box, leaving me alone in this massive fucking penthouse.

Was revenge really worth it?

After cleaning the whole penthouse and returning everything to how it was before the party, I sat on the couch waiting. I wound up falling asleep as the sun started to rise. Corvin never came home. Maybe Leah was right, I need to pack my shit and leave. I can't exactly stay in his house when I'm not welcome now, can I? I force my tired body off the couch and make my way to my room. I debate leaving the clothes he bought me behind, but decide against that idea. He did say I could do whatever I want with them and honestly, as pathetic as it sounds, having something he bought with me that I can hold and think of him seems like a great idea right now.

An hour later, I have everything packed and ready to go. I drop my bags by the entryway and look around. When I first stepped foot inside this place I was angry, and thirsted for retribution for my sister. But now, standing here and looking around at the empty space, all I feel is remorse and disgust with myself. I used him, played him like a fiddle and all he did was try to help me. I never should have set out on this path of destruction because now I finally see, my sister's death wasn't Corvin's fault. I just needed someone to blame to help me cope with the pain of the loss and he was the easiest to blame.

The sound of the elevator pinging to announce its arrival has me spinning around and hope blooming inside me that he's finally come back. The moment the doors open, all hope flees me when I see Darius standing there. He steps out of the lift and looks from me to my bags and nods.

"Come on, I'll give you a lift," is all he says before helping me carry my bags. We ride silently to the parking garage, and neither of us utters a single word as we load my bags in the back of the Range Rover, or even when we slip inside the car. He pulls out and I refuse to speak first and tell him where to go. I close my eyes and lean my head against the window, getting lost in my thoughts until the sound of my sister's voice fills the silent car. I snap my gaze to Darius but he keeps his eyes on the road as I lean over and turn up the volume.

"Corv, baby, he found Val and he's at the house. If I don't make it out of here, I want you to know that I don't regret a single moment I got to spend with you. I love you. I know you won't say it back and that's okay. I need you to do me a favor though..." Tears cascade down my cheeks as I listen to the fearful whispers of my sister. *"My little sister Alexa is going to go crazy if I die. Please don't hurt her. Help her... for me please."* I hear a woman scream in the background and then a kid whimper and my stomach drops. *"She is spiteful and will blame you, make her see this isn't your fault. She doesn't have anyone besides me, baby. Be there for*

her. I love you, Corvin." The recording cuts out and a horrible-sounding sob rips out of me. Oh God. The pain I feel inside my chest is excruciating and robs me of air. I start gasping and Darius pulls the car over but says nothing, just sits there silently, and allows me the time I need to work through the debilitating pain coursing through my body.

I don't know how much time passes before Darius finally speaks. "Look out your window, Alexa." I slowly lift my tear-filled gaze to look where he says. I gasp. I see Saint, Crue, Beckett, and Leah running around, then I see a football flying through the air and look in the direction it came from. Standing there with a smile on his face, shirtless and in a pair of low-slung basketball shorts is Corvin. I watch the five of them play football for a few minutes before I tear my gaze away and look at Darius who wears a blank expression on his face.

"Why am I here?" I ask.

"When I look at Leah, I see my future. When she smiles or laughs it makes me happy knowing she is happy. When she's upset, I get angry, I want to kill whoever the fuck made my girl sad. Being away from her for even an hour makes me angsty, she isn't just someone I'm fucking in love with, she is my reason for existing and wanting to live. Without her, I was nothing, a shell of a man if you will, but with her by my side, I can conquer the fucking world because she makes me strong." I stay silent waiting for him to explain why he is telling me this. "I know Corvin better than anyone, even his own sister." He pins me with a hard stare. I swallow audibly, knowing he is about to say some deep shit. "My boy has never lived with a chick. Cody stayed over but he never allowed her to move in. His cars have always been his babies. You fucking his up repeatedly should have pushed him over the edge, but it didn't. Corvin may not have meant to fall for you, but he did anyway. When I look out at him now, I see the same smile you do, but I guarantee if either of us were to look into his eyes, we would see the pain he hides from the others."

"What are trying to say, Darius?"

"I see the pain in your eyes, Alexa. Deny it all you want, but karma bit you in the ass because you are just as in love with him as he is with you." I stiffen in my seat. "I brought you here so you could see what he does. You'll see him around campus smiling and acting like he isn't dying inside. Don't let his act fool you."

"Why?" I whisper.

"If he's what you want and I mean what you really fucking want, you need to let go of the resentment and the past and stop blaming him. Don't fucking come for him until you are one hundred fucking percent sure you are all in, because he will risk his career for you. I won't let him do that unless I am fucking sure you won't fuck him over. He has no idea I'm even here. He wanted all of us to leave you be and let you continue to hurt him. I won't allow that to happen because my brother deserves fucking better than that. He's a good fucking guy, Alexa, and will give you every part of his heart if you let him. He may have told your sister he loved her but I'll tell you a secret—" his eyes draw me in and hold me captive, "He never looked at Cody the way he looks at you."

CHAPTER SIXTEEN

Saying goodbye to my sister and the guy's sucks. I didn't realize how fucking much I missed them until I had to watch them leave. Diving home alone blows. I have no one to distract me from my thoughts and keep my mind off the raven-haired beauty that plowed her way into my life and forced her way into my heart, only to rip it to shreds all in the name of vengeance. I debate going to see Travis and working out until I'm numb, but I know I'm just putting off the inevitable and should just get it over with now.

My hands grow clammy as I pull into the parking garage of my building. The whole ride up in the lift, I keep gnawing on my bottom lip. The doors open and I have to force myself to step out of the metal box. I round the corner into the living room slowly, looking toward the kitchen and find them both empty and clean. I expected to come home to a mess and everything smashed, so I'm pleasantly surprised that I don't have to pay cleaners or replace the furniture again. I search through the entire penthouse for her, but she's nowhere to be seen. I run back to her room and open her closet door, all the racks are empty of clothes.

My heart sinks, she's gone.

I drop down onto the edge of her bed and bury my face in the palm of my hands. "Fucking hell," I growl into the empty room before standing and storming out, slamming the door behind me. I have every intention of hunting her down until my phone pings in my pocket. I pull it out expecting it to be my sister, but freeze when I see it's from Alexa. I smile when I see the time, eleven-forty-two.

JAIL BAIT

Roses are red, Violets are blue, a face like yours belongs in a zoo, don't worry I'll be there too, not in a cage like you, but laughing at you.

Despite my sour mood, her stupid little joke has me laughing. I head over to the sofa and flop down onto it as I tap out a reply.

With a face like yours, you should sue your parents for damages.

I wait to see those three dots appear to show she is replying but no matter how long I sit here and stare at the screen they never come, and my heart aches a little more.

For the next week, I try to find her around campus but come up short. The only thing that lets me know she is okay and alive is the fact she is back to texting me at eleven-forty-two every day. When Friday rolls around, I dread it knowing I will be spending the weekend alone. Before Alexa moved in, being alone didn't bother me. I craved it but after her being with me daily, the silence of my home haunts me. I have my first game with my new team next Friday and I have to admit I'm excited about it. A part of me hopes that Alexa will come watch, but I know that's a pipedream.

Once I'm home, I grab a quick shower and order some takeout. Sitting here eating my Pad Thai as I watch ESPN, I manage to forget that I'm a lonely sack of shit until my phone lights up beside me. The moment I see her name appear on the screen, everything else is forgotten as I reach for it and swipe it open.

JAIL BAIT

> Roses are red, Violets are blue, I'm horny and want you inside me.

I reread her text at least a dozen times with my cock growing hard in my pants at the thought of being balls deep inside her.

> Don't fuck with me, jail bait.

JAIL BAIT

> Not fucking with you, I mean it. But, if you're not down.....

I type out the reply so fast I'm shocked my fingers can move that quickly.

> I'm fucking down all right! Where?

JAIL BAIT

> My dorm.

> You good with everyone hearing you scream my name?

JAIL BAIT

> LOL

JAIL BAIT

> I'll suck your cock if you can make me scream loud enough to wake my RA.

Is that a dare?

JAIL BAIT

No, it's an invitation to fuck me all night long
and make me forget about everything.

My heart lurches inside my chest. Is this another one of her games where she just needs to hurt me? I think on it for a moment but I know without a doubt, I'd let her hurt me every fucking day if I meant I got to hold her and pretend that one day she could be mine.

On my way.

JAIL BAIT

You gonna spend the night?

Can I?

Nerves thrum through me as I wait for her reply.

JAIL BAIT

Yes… now move your ass Quarter back!

I walk up the stairs to her dorm room with my duffle in my hand. The whole way here I have tried to talk myself out of doing this, knowing that this isn't going to end the way I want it to but still, I'm unable to stop myself from giving into the need to be with her. Before I can back out, I knock on her door and wait with bated breath to finally feast my gaze upon her after a week. The moment she opens the door, I drink her in. Her hair is in a messy bun atop her head, wearing a tank top and booty shorts that hug her perfectly. When I finally meet her stare, I see the same unease I feel inside myself reflected back at me in those beautiful blue eyes.

She says nothing as she steps aside and allows me to enter,

closes the door behind me and I look around her room. She has a double bed, a tiny walk-in closet on one side of the room, and a desk and dresser on the other side. I know she has her own bathroom in here. I made sure of it because I didn't want her sharing with anyone, or risk some sleazy fucker breaking in and snooping on her in the shower. I want to pat myself on the back for having the forethought of making sure she got a single room and didn't have to share or this booty call wouldn't be happening here right now. I spot some photos on the corkboard above her desk. I drop my bag and make my way over to get a better look.

I feel her gaze boring into the back of my head the whole way. A smile tugs at my lips seeing a picture of her and Cody together. There's a photo of Cody, me, Saint, Crue and Katie that was taken at the cabin last Christmas. The one picture that draws my attention to it is the one of her and me in my bed. I'm asleep with half my face nestled into her hair and my arm wrapped possessively around her waist. I look beside it and my eyes widen. It's another picture of me but this time it's of me in my WFU uniform training. She must have taken this one of the nights she was waiting for me to finish practice and I had no idea. I pull the picture of me and her off and turn back to face her, she doesn't drop her gaze from mine.

"Why did you take this?" I ask quietly.

"Reaper—"

"Don't lie to me," I snap.

"If you want me to tell you then I will, but you leave straight after. I asked you here for one reason. I made my intentions clear like you did with Cod—" She clamps her mouth and takes a deep breath.

"So… this is just sex then?"

She nibbles on her bottom lips and nods stiffly. "Yes." I stuff the photo in my back pocket before I slowly prowl toward her. I leave an inch of space between us. I love the way her breathing speeds up and her eyes turn glassy. I reach out, graze the tips of my fingers up her bare arms slowly, goose bumps begin to dot her skin.

"You want me to fuck you but we can't talk?"

She swallows and nods her head as I reach the tops of her shoulders. "Y-yeah."

"You gonna let me fuck you however I want?" I whisper as I slowly lean down and ghost my lips over hers.

"However, you want," she answers breathlessly.

"Good girl, now get the fuck on the bed." Her eyes blaze with raw unfiltered need as I put space between us and wait for her to follow my demands. She stands at the edge of the bed and looks directly at me as she pushes her booty shorts down to reveal a tiny lace thong. I grind my teeth and clench my hands at my sides. She rids herself of the tank top, letting her full tits free. Fuck, they are perfect and perky, her nipples beginning to harden and my mouth waters begging me for a taste. She turns, giving me the best fucking view of her pert ass as she crawls up the bed, turns over and rests back against the pillows looking to me for the next instruction. I stalk toward her, loving the way her eyes drink me in. I stop at the foot of the bed and reach behind my neck, gripping my shirt and pulling it off. Her greedy eyes take in my exposed skin. I grip the waistband of my shorts and push them down. Her eyes drop to my boxers and a small whimper escapes her at the sight of my hard cock straining to get free. "Open your legs."

She does exactly as I say and I relish the sight of the damp spot I see on her lacy thong. She can pretend she doesn't want me, but her body betrays her every time. I hop on the bed and crawl toward her, run my hands up her legs, stopping at her waist. I grip her and yank her down to me, loving the gasp that slips free. Her lace-covered pussy is flush against my cotton covered cock. She tries to push down against it but I hold her still.

"Corvin—"

"Shut the fuck up, Alexa," I growl. Any other time she would mouth back at me but right now, she needs me knowing I am the only one who can rip her apart and bring her back together again. I glide my hands further up her body and cup her tits. Her back arches off the bed as a small cry leaves her sinful mouth. I roll her nipples between my fingers loving the way she squirms beneath me. I thrust my hips forward making sure my cock hits her clit, she cries out.

"Fuck, Corvin, please just fuck me." I release her tits and grip the back of her neck, pulling her up halfway as I lean down until our foreheads are touching.

"You got to fuck with me and now I'm going to take whatever the fuck I want from you and you're going to let me." I don't wait for her to answer, I smash my lips to hers and force her back until she is lying flat on the bed. I moan at the taste of her. She wraps her arms around my neck and deepens the kiss. I grind my cock into her and swallow the moan that tumbles from her. I tear my lips from hers and trail kisses down her neck and chest until I reach her tits. I suck one of her nipples into my mouth and swirl my tongue around it, loving the sounds that come from her. I switch sides, paying the other the same amount of attention before continuing to lick a trail down her stomach. I slip off the end of the bed and drop to my knees. I grip her ankles and yank her down until her pussy is right in my face. I run my tongue along the inside of her thigh, she shivers in anticipation. Then I brush my lips over the tiny triangle that shields her pussy from me.

"Oh fuck," she breathes out when I lick her through the lace. I grip her thong and peel it down her legs. She rests up on her elbows and watches me ball them up, bring it to my nose and inhale her heady scent.

"Fuck, you smell so good, baby," I growl.

"I taste even better," she huskily taunts as she reaches down and runs her fingers through my hair, then pushes my head forward until my face is buried in her dripping cunt.

CHAPTER SEVENTEEN

Alexa

"Fuck!" I cry out when he sucks my clit into his mouth. Corvin doesn't tease or try to prolong this, he feasts on my pussy like a starved man. I honestly didn't think I would cave and text him to come over, but the thought of sleeping with someone else had my stomach rolling at the thought of letting someone else touch me like this. Not being able to talk to him all week aside from my daily texts has sucked. The only time I've gotten to see him is when he is at practice and I hide like a stalker, watching him train with his team for their first game next week.

The moment he pushes a finger inside me, I drop back onto the bed and cry out. He works me up into a frenzy. I pinch my nipples and shudder. Fuck, his mouth feels so fucking amazing against my pussy. I haven't been able to get myself off all week. It's like my own body knows that Corvin is the only one who can make us come harder than we ever have before. He adds a second finger and I'm done.

"Fuck, I'm coming!" I scream out as my back arches off the bed and pleasure tears through my whole body. Aftershocks rip through me as he laps at my pussy, gently bringing me down slowly from the most incredible high.

"Fuck, I love your cunt," he growls as he stands and leans over the bed, hovering his face above mine. I don't wait for him to make the first move. I snake my arms around his neck and pull his mouth down to mine. Fuck, the taste of my release mixed with the taste of him has me moaning. Tasting myself on him has a sense of possessiveness coursing through me, I want to be the only woman he tastes and that thought shocks the fuck out of me. He breaks the kiss and straightens as he pushes his boxers down his legs. His cock springs free, slapping against his stomach. My mouth waters at the sight of pre cum. "Get on your knees now, jail bait." He doesn't have to tell me twice.

I kneel in front of him on the floor, lift my gaze to his and open my mouth. The moment I taste him, heat spreads through my body. I've sucked dick before and hated the taste, but sucking Corvin's cock isn't something I dread the thought of. The taste of him is addictive. I grip the base of his cock and pump him as I begin to bob my head up and down on his thick cock.

"Fuck, baby, take it all the way like a good girl." I do as he says and relax my throat as I slowly work my way down his cock. I feel him in my throat and fuck me, it's an intoxicating feeling. "Fuck yes. God, I love how you don't have a gag reflex. You're fucking perfect," he grits out as he tangles his hand in my messy bun. He takes over then and begins to fuck my face. I have to grip his thighs for something to hang on to. The other times we've fucked he's never been this rough, but fuck, seeing him lose control and take whatever the fuck he wants from me has me growing wetter by the second. He rips his cock out of my mouth and I gasp for air as spit drips down my chin and chest. "Get on the fucking bed and open those legs like a good girl so I can see *my* pussy." The possessive tone of his voice has a shiver rolling through me and the need to obey him is urgent. I do exactly as he says and love the growl of approval that comes from him as he stares down at my wet cunt.

He slowly crawls up my body, resting his hands on either side of my head. I feel the head of his cock prodding at my entrance and hold my breath in anticipation. He slowly pushes inside me—he doesn't rush, he wants me to feel every fucking inch of him slipping inside me. Emotions begin to swirl inside me as I look into those brown eyes of his, he doesn't shield his emotions from me and allows me to see it. I can see it clear as day, Darius was right, and Corvin Williams is in love with me.

"Fuck," he grits out the moment he is fully sheathed inside me. I'm woman enough to admit that I feel complete with him balls deep inside me. The feelings I have been fighting try to surface. I force them back down, not wanting to allow them to ruin this moment. Corvin must sense the shift in me as his eyes soften a fraction before his lips are on mine, drawing me out of my own thoughts and forcing me to focus on nothing else but him and the way he is making me feel. He begins to move inside, pulling a gasp from me that forces us to break the kiss. He keeps his face an inch above mine, holding my gaze as he thrusts inside me. The last time we had sex, he switched positions so he didn't have to look at me but now, he wants me to see everything he's feeling.

A cry forces its way past my lips when he hits that sweet spot inside me. "Oh fuck, keep doing that." He obeys my demand and hits that spot over and over again, driving me fucking crazy. I need him to fuck me hard but he's deter-mined to take his time and—-holy shit, it slots into place for me. Corvin isn't fucking me, he's making love to me and that realization has tears clouding my vision.

"Tell me this pussy is mine and I'll make you come," he forces out through clenched teeth. I gape up at him. The bastard just smirks knowingly, he hasn't made me come on purpose!

"No." He doesn't stop fucking me, just keeping to his steady pace. My orgasm is right there, cresting on the horizon but I can't latch onto it no matter how hard I try. I will go fucking crazy soon if he doesn't fuck me hard and force me over the edge, but my pride won't allow me to relent and say what he wants.

"Admit it's mine, jail bait, and I'll fuck you senseless." I grit my teeth to keep from blurting out what he wants to hear. A primal cry rips out of me when thrusts inside me so hard I shift up the bed. Fuck, my body begins to quiver from the pressure building inside. When he pulls back I wait for him to do it again, knowing this time I'll come, but he stills and looks down at me waiting. "You don't want to admit that this is more than sex, fine. But, if you want my cock inside this pussy you're going to admit it's mine or I'll walk out of here and leave you on edge all fucking night. You and I both know there is only one cock you want, baby, and it's mine. Make your choice."

Fuck!

I'm too strung out and from the look in his eyes, I know without a doubt he means what he says and will walk out. "Fine, it's yours," I scream at him, equal parts hating myself but also loving the way it feels to admit he owns a part of me.

"What's mine?" he taunts.

I narrow my eyes. "This pussy is yours, now fuck it and make me come, Reaper." His eyes blaze as his chest puffs out slightly, knowing he won that round. Gripping each of my legs he places them on his shoulders, then pushes forward until my feet rest on either side of my head and slams his cock all the way inside forcing a strangled cry from my lips.

"Scream my fucking name, jail bait," he grits out as he begins to fuck me at a brutal pace. He's so deep and fuck me, I'm powerless to stop the orgasm that tears through me.

"Corvin!" I scream so fucking loud, it echo's around the room. Before I can come down from my high, he pulls out and flips me onto my stomach, pushing me to my knee's a moment before he's fucking me from behind. Holy fuck. Him fucking me doggy has a whole new lot of sensations racing through me. His balls smack against my clit and I moan. His grip on my waist is punishing. I know I'll have bruises tomorrow and that thought has me moaning and slamming back into him, loving the hiss that comes from him.

"Fuck yeah, baby," he breathes out as he grips my hair and uses it to pull me up until my back is plastered against his chest. One of his arms bands around my waist and the other clamps around my neck. I turn my head to the side and peer up at him. The frenzied look in his brown eyes has my pussy clamping down on his cock. He snaps his gaze to mine a second before his mouth is on mine. I meet him thrust for thrust, moaning into his mouth as I feel another climax building. He breaks the kiss and stares deep into my eyes as he growls, "Come with me, jail bait. I need to feel my pussy strangling the life out of my cock." His words are my undoing, one more thrust and I'm sent tumbling over the edge with his name on my lips. He follows after me, roaring my name loud enough to wake every student on this floor. We flop forward, utterly spent. He rolls us to our sides with his cock still buried inside me and nuzzles his face into the crook of my neck. "Good girl."

A shiver runs through me. I didn't think I was the type of girl who liked to be praised whilst being fucked but clearly, I was wrong. Hearing him call me a good girl has me wanting to do whatever it takes just to hear him say it again and again. Jesus. A pit forms in my stomach, this really isn't just sex anymore.

🏈

Waking up wrapped in Corvin's arms the past two mornings feels incredible. He was only supposed to stay Friday night, but then Saturday morning I woke to his face between my legs and of course, the need to suck his cock overcame me. We ended up in bed all day fucking, watching movies, and just… hanging out. It was weird, before there was this secret between us and now that everything is out in the open, it feels… different.

Corvin's grip around my waist tightens and I smile as he begins to pepper kisses along my naked shoulder. "Why are you up so early?" His voice is raspy from sleep and fuck the sound of it has a shiver rolling through me and my pussy growing slick. I push back into him and moan when I feel his hard cock prodding against my lower back.

"Fuck me." Two words. That's all it takes for Corvin to have me on my back and himself nestled between my legs with his cock prodding at my entrance. I hold my breath, waiting to feel every inch of him disappear inside me. A knock sounds at the fucking door, drawing both of our attention to it.

"Expecting someone?" Corv asks. I wrack my brain trying to think but it's pretty fucking hard when I have his cock pressed against my entrance.

"I-I don't know." He nods and leaps off me. I pout as I watch him pull on his boxers, grabs his shirt off the floor and flings it at me. I quickly pull it over my head and draw the covers over my legs, he runs his gaze over me once more to make sure I'm covered before he opens the door.

Oh shit.

Corvin's shoulders bunch and I tense in my bed. "The fuck are you doing here?" Corvin snaps. I'm so not getting laid now.

CHAPTER EIGHTEEN

My grip on the door tightens at the sight of Ash standing there wearing his Sunday best. He runs his gaze over me and his face scrunched in disgust before he looks inside and spots Alexa. I shift and hide her from his view, which brings us almost chest to chest with a sliver of space between our bodies. He takes a step back shaking his head with a smile. I still, waiting for him to attack or say something dumb—he does neither of those. Instead he stands tall and holds my gaze as he speaks.

"I should have known."

"Known what?" I grit out.

He smiles sadly and that throws me. "When she asked me to breakfast it was only a ploy to get at you." I keep the hurt off my face. He shoves his hands in his pockets and shrugs his shoulders. "I didn't realize you two were still a thing. That's my bad, bro, and I assure you *this* won't happen again." He doesn't wait for a reply as he turns and walks away. It takes me a couple seconds to gather myself and push down the hurt inside me.

She told me this was just sex. My dumb ass thought the fact she came to me and not someone else meant she was finally coming around to admitting that she fucking has feelings for me as well, but obviously I was fucking wrong! I close the door and turn around, but I can't look at her. I head straight to my bag, grab out a shirt and my pants, then dress as quickly as I can so I can get the fuck out of here. I'm zipping my duffle up when her hand lands on my wrist. I jump back and glare down at her.

"Don't touch me," I grit out. Hurt flashes in her blue eyes before she quickly masks it. Standing here and looking down at her in *my* shirt, her hair a mess from us fucking all night and she had hickeys lining either side of her neck, my way of showing every other fucker that she is mine. What a fucking fool I am. She was never mine and I was a fucking idiot for allowing myself to think otherwise.

"Would you just let me explain?" she begs. I shake my head, unable to stand here and hear her bullshit excuses.

"It was just sex, right?" She flinches. I sound like an asshole, but right now I don't give a shit. I reach into the side pocket of my duffle and pull out the ticket I got her for next Friday's game and toss it on the bed. She frowns at the sight of it before looking back at me. "My dumbass thought after spending the night with me you would change your mind about us. I got you the ticket so you could come to the game as my girlfriend." I laugh but there is no humor, it's just pain. Her face is a picture of shock and that just pisses me off. "I never should have come here. I was a fucking idiot. You told me this was all a game to you and still I fucking hoped you would change your mind and see that I'm not the bad guy here. I'm fucking sorry about Cody dying, Alexa. I never wanted that shit to happen and I hate myself for any part I played in it. The thing is, what I want with you I never wanted with your sister." Her eyes widen, I see moisture beginning to build in her eyes.

She shakes her head. "It's not that simple, you can't just expect me to forget everything!" she yells.

"I don't expect you to forget anything. All I wanted was for you to give me a chance to show you I'm not the monster you think I am." Tears slowly leak from her eyes and my heart aches at the sight. I need to get the fuck out of here. "If you show up to the game wearing this." I reach inside my bag and pull out my spare jersey and toss it on the bed. "I get what I want and believe me, Alexa, I fucking want you. If you don't show, I get it. I'll never bother you again and leave you alone to live your life." I place a kiss on her forehead and force my feet to move, walking away from her like this is one of the hardest fucking things I've ever had to do in my life. I open the door ready to step out, but pause when she speaks.

"She was my sister, Corvin. What you are saying to me is what she wanted from you! Why am I different? Why couldn't you just have given her this?" The anguish in her voice keeps me from turning back to face her. I keep my voice steady as I answer.

"Because I didn't love her the way she wanted me to. I cared about her a lot and wanted the best for her but now, I know I never really loved her."

"How could you know that?" I turn to peer over my shoulder at her, tears leaking from her eyes like a broken faucet.

"Because I'm in love with you." Her jaw slackens as her eyes widen in surprise, hearing those words come from my mouth. "I love you that much I'd allow you to continue to ruin my cars, trash my house, and fuck with me because I would either get messages from you to gloat or at the very least see you. I love you, Alexa, and because of that reason, I'm going to walk away now and leave everything up to you. You can either continue to live your life alone, knowing you fucking broke me and that you got your much-needed revenge. Or, you can come to that game and admit... you love me too."

Five days

I check my phone for the hundredth time, hoping she would have called or texted by now but of course, she is too fucking stubborn. I thought about going radio silent and leaving her to work things out in her own head. Coming home Sunday to an empty house sucked. I've never wanted a girl with me all hours of the fucking day, but Alexa, I want her with me everywhere I go. I know if I get drafted that is going to be fucking hard because she still has school and I'd have to travel, but honestly, I'd do anything to make it work with her. This may have all been a game to her and yeah, she played me like a fucking fool, but she won the grand prize. She owns my heart and I don't want it back. Which is why when I didn't hear from her all day Sunday or Monday morning, I decided to message her at eleven-forty-two every day. I scroll through my messages and re-read the ones I sent her. I told her every day this week things I noticed about her that no one else would have, unless they were watching her constantly, like me. I even set the photo I took of her and me in bed on Saturday morning as my screensaver.

> You scrunch your nose and narrow your eyes when you concentrate.

> You like it when I kiss you just below your ear, it sends shivers down your spine and turns you on.

> Watching you smile as you daydream has become one of my favorite sights to see.

> Seeing you across campus today with your friends and watching you laugh so freely made me happy. You deserve your happiness, jail bait, even if it isn't with me.

I stare down at the last message I sent her today and a part of me wishes I never sent it but I also know, I had to shoot my last shot.

> Game Day, baby. I wish I knew if you were coming or not. Having you there would mean the fucking world to me, but I also get it if you don't show. If I don't see you at the game tonight, this will be the last message you will ever get from me. I'll keep my word and not bother you. If this is the last time I get to talk to you, then I need you to know something. Cody loved you, Alexa, and she only wanted what was best for you. I want what is best for you. I love you, jail bait and fuck, I hope I get to see you tonight.

I'm man enough to admit that I am fucking miserable without her. I've never depended on someone to bring me joy or the need for happiness. I was perfectly content with having my boys by my side and partying it up. Fuck, I was fine with fucking a different chick each night until Cody came along. She and I weren't ideal and I know that now. We fought too much and honestly, in the end, I think we knew we had grown apart. She wanted a ring and a white picket fence, I just wanted to live my life and have fun until I was drafted.

I was stupid and selfish. I know that now because the roles are reversed and I'm the one wanting something with Alexa. She and I are fucking toxic, I know that and so does she but it's only because she can't let go of the past and stop blaming me! I know if she does, she won't feel so much guilt for loving me. Five days without her feels like a lifetime. I miss her sassy attitude and her snarky replies. I miss the smell of her hair and even the way she rolls her eyes when I call her jail bait. Every night this week, I've jerked off to the memory of her telling me that her pussy is mine. I fucking pray that she comes tonight, because if she doesn't, I doubt my heart will ever recover from losing someone like her. Alexa isn't like every other girl, she is different and so unapologetically her. She has me eating out of the palm of her hand and I'm not even mad about it.

All I need is for her to admit those three little words aloud. I just hope Karma doesn't get me and she waits till I die to say them.

"All you ladies better hustle out there! I don't want to see any fumbled passes, no drop balls or I'll make sure the lot you wish you never had balls to begin with." I smirk, Travis really fucking sucks at pre game speeches. I look around the locker room at my new team and smile. I have faith in them, we got this shit in the bag. They gave me a hard time, but the more I proved myself and my worth to the team, the less they gave me shit. They know I can bring home the W tonight. "Corvin." I snap my gaze to Travis and quirk a brow. "You fucking throw like you have never thrown before. If you throw a Hail Mary, you make sure it's in the fucking endzone, got it?" I smile and nod.

"I got this," I say cockily. The team cheers and shouts. I join in on the excitement but the moment Travis tells Ash to lead the team from the locker room, my stomach twists into knots as nerves start to course through me at the prospect of seeing her or not. By the end of tonight I could have a girl-friend or wind up broken hearted. I follow the team out, the vibe in the tunnel as we make our way to the field is unlike any other. It's this moment right here that sets the stage for the whole game. If you don't have the mojo within the team as you walk out, then your game will bomb, it's an unwritten fact of the game.

"Let's do this, boys!" Ash screams from the front. He and I have actually hung out a couple times during practice and I have to admit he isn't a dick like I thought. He's actually a really good guy. I follow after the team and the moment we step out of the tunnel and the crowd sees us they go crazy and cheer. The announcers start to introduce me and I hold my helmet so they all know who the new starting QB is.

"Corvin Williams is the starting quarterback for WFU for the remainder of the season. Captain and star QB Asher Nolls sustained an injury and Corvin stepped in. The guy's stats are amazing and his win record with CHU is impressive. Wake Forest University is proud to introduce its new starting QB, give it up for Corvin Williams!" The crowd goes wild at the announcer's introduction. It's then that I finally lift my gaze and look toward the seat where I pray Alexa is sitting.

A smile stretches across my face at the sight of my sister, Darius, Beckett, Val, Dawson, Crue and Saint. The guys had a by-game this week and I honestly didn't expect to see any of them here tonight! Crue and Saint lift a sign above their heads. It's bright freaking orange and stands out like a sore thumb.

WFU's QB is the best at handling balls, just ask us!

I shake my head, they are fucking idiots! Before making my way over to them I run my gaze to the other end of the row and the smile drops off my face. The seat she's meant to be in remains vacant. My heart sinks in my chest and any teether of hope I still held onto dissipates. I swore off relationships after Lana, promising myself I would never let another girl get close enough to fuck with my head or hurt me. Yet, I unknowingly allowed Alexa full access to all of me. I fell in love with a girl who never had any intentions of loving me back. My chest burns knowing I lost her.

Closing my eyes, I force the feeling of my heart breaking inside my chest down. All I need to do is get through tonight and win the game. I'll deal with everything else tomorrow because tonight, I plan to mend my heart by finding my way to the bottom of a bottle of Patron.

CHAPTER NINETEEN

Alexa

Six days later

"You really didn't have to drive me around you know." Katie looks over and smiles at me. She's been the only person I have been able to speak to about everything where Corvin is concerned. I flew out here last night, we have four days over Easter and I know Corvin is at his cabin with his friends. Katie refused to go because her, Saint and Crue are still not speaking, so she stayed back with Nathan.

"I know, but it's not like I have much else to do," she says solemnly.

"They still won't let you explain?" I push. She sighs and shakes her head.

"No. It's okay though, I made the mistake and now I have to live with my choices but I do need to tell you something." I tense.

"Why does it sound bad?"

She smiles but it doesn't reach her eyes. "It won't matter to you since you live in NC, but I'm heading back home. I enrolled in a local college back there."

"What the fuck! Why?"

She shrugs her shoulders as we pull up out front of the place I have refused to visit. "One day I may just tell you, but for now, I don't want you keeping a secret from Corvin that isn't yours to keep, if you get what I mean?" I frown but say nothing. As I get out of the car and make the trek across the cemetery, I know if I truly am to move on, then this is something I need to do. The moment I see her tombstone a lump forms in my throat.

Cody Alice Sutton

Seeing her name written in stone has tears clouding my vision. I've avoided coming here, as the fact of seeing her name displayed on this fucking stone makes it real. She's never coming back, no matter the amount of pain I inflict on Corvin or anyone else. My sister is gone and I need to face that fact, or I risk sabotaging my own chance at happiness. Lowering to my knees, I reach out and brush my fingers across her name.

"I miss you so much," I choke out. "I know you can probably see the mess I've made from up there but I swear, Cody, I only meant to honor our pact, not fall for your sort-of boyfriend." Shame washes over me admitting that aloud. Corvin was right, I do have feelings for him. I had planned to go to his game and show him that I wanted more with him, but receiving his texts each day, I knew if I wanted to give this thing with him a shot, a real shot, then I needed to let go of the past and stop blaming him. "I know you're probably pissed at me and I get it. I would be too but I… I love him, Cody, and I want to be with him." Saying that aloud for the first time has a weight lifting off my chest. I had no idea how freeing it would feel to finally stop lying to myself about my feelings. "I came here to tell you that I choose him. I love him and I know it will be hard if he gets drafted and me being at school, but I just know we can make it work. I'm so sorry, Cody. I love you and miss you, sister, but I can't let him go."

◆

After spending an hour talking to Cody and crying myself out of tears, I say goodbye and head back to the car where Katie waits for me. She smiles and reaches out to place her hand on my shoulder when I slip into the car.

"She would be so fucking proud of you, Lexi." Her words have my eyes welling with tears again. I reach and pull her hand from my shoulder and clasp it in mine as I look directly into her eyes so she can see how serious I am.

"Thank you for always checking on me and being kind even when I was a bitch to you." Her bottom lip trembles. "You are an amazing friend and my sister was so lucky to have you."

"You have me as well, Lexi."

I smile. "I know, which is why I need to ask a favor, please."

"Of course." I tell her my plan and I see she is hesitant to do it and run the risk of running into certain people, but in the end, she finally agrees. Nervous energy courses through me as we head back to CHU so we can pick Nathan up, but I have another idea first.

"Can you take me to the house where she... died." Katie eyes me skeptically for a beat.

"Are you sure that's a good idea?" she asks cautiously.

"I need to let shit go and if that house is a part of his life, I need to see it. Please, Katie."

She sighs and nods. "Okay."

◆

We pull up out front of a two-story home. Yellow tape still covers the patio and I begin to rethink my decision as Katie parks her car in the empty driveway. The moment she kills the ignition, all that can be heard is my own heavy breathing. My palms begin to grow clammy and I have to rub them on my jeans a couple times.

"Lexi, you don't have to do this," she says gently. I shake my head, keeping my gaze on the front of the house.

"Why is there still tape?" I ask. I see her shoulders deflate as she takes a shuddering breath and looks in the direction of the house.

"No one has been back here since the day after. The guys packed everything and never came back."

"Why?"

"They all left it up to Corvin on what to do with the house. He hasn't come back here since that night and I honestly don't think he plans to, but it's not like they are out of pocket leaving it vacant or anything." I snort, of course not, they are all fucking loaded.

"Do you have a key?" I ask as I get out of the car. Katie follows my lead and gets out.

"I know where the spare is." She leads the way up the path. I force each foot in front of the other. Katie climbs the steps and comes to a stop just before the yellow tape. I peer around her to see bunches of flowers and soft toys people have left here. The dead can't do shit with the flowers or a teddy bear, I never saw the point in that shit. Ducking under the tape I watch as Katie lifts a plant in the corner and pulls a key out. The moment the lock clicks open, we both still for a second before she pushes the door open. I follow her in and look around. The house smells like… I can't even describe it really. Dust covers everything which further confirms she is right, no one has been here in months.

I don't look around as I follow Katie past the living room, into the kitchen and head into another room that looks like a rumpus slash games room. Katie freezes in the doorway. I push past her and step further into the room, coming to a stop at the sight on the floor. Gauze, gloves and other things from the EMTs remain on the floor, but it's the brownish stain on it that pulls my focus. This is where Cody took her last breath.

"He held her and tried to stop the bleeding. He was covered in her blood, Lexi. He was the first to perform CPR and even after the paramedics pronounced her dead, he took over and continued to try and revive her. Corvin stayed with her the entire time until the coroner turned up and asked him to step out. Even when they were taking her out, he stopped them and told her he loved her again." Tears slowly trail down my cheeks. "He held her and told her everything she wanted to hear. The sounds that came from him when he finally accepted that she was gone will haunt me for the rest of my life."

I slowly turn around to face her and ask, "Why are you telling me this?"

Her features harden. "Because you are full of shit." I balk at her. "You didn't need to come here to let go of shit, you're just trying to find any excuse not to admit you are in love with the same guy your sister was. Cody is gone, Alexa. She isn't coming back to claim Corvin, but you can. You can claim your man, but you need to pull your fucking head out of your ass and stop punishing yourself and him for something neither of you could have stopped. It was a horrific accident. Let it go and move on, Lexi. It's what she would want and you know that."

Hearing the truth out loud fucking stings like a bitch.

●

"Wake up." I jolt awake in my seat and stare out the window to see it's dark out. I look at the time on the clock on the dash, shit, it's nine o'clock at night. I look over to Katie who seems uneasy about being here and I feel like an ass for making her drive me out here to the cabin when I know she doesn't want to see Saint and Crue.

"So, you gonna go get your man or what, boo?" I look back at Nathan and smirk. He is a fucking good time and honestly, I envy these girls for being able to call him their friend.

"Yeah, I am," I say with such conviction I surprise myself. Nathan leans forward and gives me a hug, then I hug Katie. "Thank you for everything."

She smiles lovingly and winks. "Get out of here before they see my headlights." I nod and thank them both again before getting out. I refused to allow them to drive back to CHU tonight, so I managed to nab a hotel an hour away from here for them. I watch Katie and Nathan drive away before I turn back to the mansion of a cabin. Three cars sit here in the driveway and I recognize none of them. I take a deep breath and begin to walk up the path. The moment I climb the porch steps a light flicks on and then the front door is yanked open. I come to a stop at the site of Leah standing in the doorway.

"Alexa?" If her face didn't give away her shock at the sight of me, her tone sure did.

"Uh, hey?" I say awkwardly, the last time we saw each other wasn't exactly pleasant so there is tension thrumming between us.

"Babe?" I hear someone call out a second before Darius appears beside Leah. At the sight of me his brows jump to his hairline. "What the fuck," he breathes out.

This is so fucking awkward, why couldn't Corvin have just answered the door! "Uh, is Corvin around?" I ask hesitantly. Darius frowns, looking confused. Leah on the other hand looks murderous. Yippee.

"He isn't here," she forces out through clenched teeth.

"What?" Leah has to be full of shit, he told me himself this is where he would be spending Easter and it's Good Friday.

"Corvin got drafted, Alexa." I stare at Darius completely thrown off by his declaration.

I shake my head denying his claim. "He can't, he just played—"

Leah cuts me off before I can finish. "How the fuck would you know? My brother told me you never showed. He also told all of us the choice he gave you and yet here you fucking stand. Was breaking his heart not enough? Oh wait, let me guess you need more money, right?" My mouth drops open, anger thrums through me at her accusation.

"Goldie!" Darius tries to warn his girlfriend, but I ignore him as I meet her angry glare with one of my own.

"I was at the fucking game, miss thang! I just watched from a different section. Just so we are clear, I never asked your brother for a fucking cent of his money, so don't fucking judge me when you don't know shit about me!"

"I know that you love to fuck with my brother's head and I won't fucking let you do it again, or ruin this opportunity for him!" She closes the space between us, and thanks to our raised voices, Saint, Crue, Beck, and Valance now stand in the doorway behind Darius.

"Fuck you, Leah," I snarl. "You told me not to come back for him unless I was all in. Well I'm here because I want him and I'm laying all my cards on the fucking table for your brother, you uptight snob. But I guess you lucked out; he isn't here and I fucking fumbled that ball badly, didn't I?"

"Yeah, you fucking did! You should have pulled your head out of your ass sooner and realized what an amazing fucking guy you had, but nooo, you just had to think you were better than him. Newsflash, you wannabe Wednesday Adams, you're not! Corvin is ten times better than you–"

"Fuck you!" I scream.

"Kiss my ass, Wednesday! You fucking destroyed him and now it's my duty as his sister to do the same to you." I stand tall and wait for her to throw a punch or something.

"You really thought showing up here and admitting you loved him would make everything you put him through okay?" Saint asks. I can tell the question is rhetorical so I remain silent. Saint pushes his way through the others to come stand beside Leah, the look in his eyes tells me I'm his least favorite person and I can't say I'm surprised. "How the fuck did you even find this place?"

I nibble on my bottom lip and debate if I should I tell them the truth or not. His eyes narrow in warning. "A friend brought me." Crue curses under his breath and comes out to stand beside Saint, his gaze drills into mine.

"Katie was here, wasn't she?" he bites out.

"Yes," I breathe out, hating that I ratted on my friend.

"Where is she?" Crue demands. I stand tall and hold my head high as I answer.

"I can't tell you. If you want to know, then you need to call her. I'm not getting involved in your… situation?" I voice it as a question because honestly, I have no idea what the three of them are and it's none of my damn business.

Leah snorts, drawing my attention back to her. "So, you do have a heart." I scowl at the blonde bombshell. She may look innocent and sweet, but the girl is a savage.

"Shockingly, yes," I snap.

"Where was that heart when you were destroying my brother's?"

Guilt rears its ugly head inside me. "It was with my sister." Her features falter for a second before she firms her mask and keeps her face free of emotion. "I'm sorry, Leah. I was wrong for doing what I did to Corvin, I had no right to hurt him the way I did. I was angry and hurt, I just lost the one person in this whole fucking world who actually gave a shit about me. I needed someone to blame and…"

"Corvin was the easiest target," she tacks on for me. I nod. "You ever hurt my brother again, Alexa, I will fucking flay you alive. I can't forgive you for what you put him through, but I also won't be the one who stands in the way of my brother's happiness. Fuck knows why out of all the women in the world he chose to fall for you. He could have done better, if you ask me." My chest rises and falls, but the pain inside almost robs me of air. I refuse to break down in front of all of them. I spin around and prepare to walk my ass to the nearest bus stop and get the fuck out of this place and never come back.

"Wait!" I pause and peer over my shoulder, she's nibbling her bottom lip, looking torn between wanting to rip my hair out and helping me, I pray for the latter. She eyes me up and down for a minute before a whoosh of air escapes her. "Where's your luggage?"

I frown at her odd question. "The airline lost it."

She rolls her eyes. "Fine, you can use Corvin's clothes he left in his room, I don't like you enough to share mine with you." I scrunch my face in confusion. She throws her hands in the air, exasperated with me. "Get your ass inside. You can stay with us until we figure out a way to get Corvin here." Hope sparks inside me.

CHAPTER TWENTY

Alexa

Four weeks later

I spent Easter weekend with Leah and the others at their cabin, trying to formulate a plan that would get Corvin there, but when Darius called him, he didn't answer. The others tried and were sent straight to voicemail. Sunday finally rolled around, and Darius received a text from him saying that he wasn't allowed his phone at training camp. Needless to say, I left them all downstairs and locked myself in Corvin's room and cried. Leah and I are on speaking terms, but I wouldn't exactly call us *friends*—we're more like frenemies. Saint and Crue took off Saturday morning to hunt down Katie and Nathan, but returned later that night looking dejected and guilty. Darius and Beck were kind, Val was welcoming and really sweet. She texts me every couple of days to check in. I've heard from Leah a couple times, which blew my mind, but she seems to know how to humble me by tacking on an insult at the end of every text message.

That weekend gave me a chance to get to know the girls and guys better, but it still felt weird being there without Corvin. I fucking miss him. When I landed back in North

Carolina on Monday night after Easter, I went straight to the penthouse only to find it empty. I stayed there that night, hoping he would only be away for the weekend. Then one night turned into three and three turned into a week. After the second week of him not showing up, I stopped staying there and went back to my dorm.

I should have stayed at his house and never come back to school.

"Sweet juice." I clench my hands into fists at my side and take a deep calming breath. Only two more weeks of school before the summer break and then I can get the fuck out of here and away from his royal fuck-hole. I ignore him as I push through the doors of the building that houses my English class. I hope to lose him in the crowd, but no such luck. He slides up beside me and I do my best to ignore him as best as I can. The week after Easter break, he showed up in my class with Shannon, I nearly died at the sight of him. "Baby, how long are you gonna ignore me for?" I slam to a halt and turn to face the monster from my past. His face is covered in sores from the drugs. His once vibrant blue eyes are dull and devoid of any spark. His blond hair used to be styled perfectly and never had a hair out of place, but now, he just looks like a hot mess.

"Until you tell me why the fuck you are here, Jason?" He admitted that he tracked my phone. He isn't even a student here and claims to be taking a gap year, but I don't buy it.

"I missed you." He tries to reach for me, but I jump backward narrowly missing crashing into another student passing us.

"Bullshit. Why the hell are you here? Don't fucking lie to me, Jason, because I know you and you didn't come all the way out here for me."

"Sweet juice." I cringe at his stupid pet name for me, I'll take being called jail bait any day.

"Stop calling me that!" I hiss loud enough to gather the attention of other students milling about.

"I came here for you, baby. No one else, just you. I love you." I stare at him like he is out of his fucking mind.

I snort. "Your love got me black eyes, fractured bones, and bruises every other week. I'd rather finger fuck myself for the rest of my life than ever consider going back to a piece of shit like you," I seethe before I leave him standing there with a stunned look on his face. I'm glad I took Corvin's advice all those weeks ago. I refuse to allow Jason any power over me.

After my altercation with Jason this morning, I thought the day would drag on but it didn't. I was barely able to focus in my classes today. I couldn't find any excitement in rebuilding the project car in class today, nothing seems to make me happy these days. I stalk his profile on social media I hate that he's so popular that his account is even fucking verified with that stupid blue tick. I bring up the recent photo he posted of him working out without a shirt on. Over ten thousand likes and four thousand comments. Groaning, I shove my phone back into my pocket and round the corner to my dorm building, only to come to a halt at the sight of Jason sitting there on the steps.

He snaps his head up and locks eyes with me, climbs to his feet and makes his way over. This time when I look into his eyes I see desperation. I shake my head as everything finally falls into place.

"Your parents cut you off because you wouldn't go to rehab?" It's posed a question but I honestly don't need him to answer because I know I'm right.

"I just need some help to get back on my feet—" I stumble back a couple steps, staring at him in utter disbelief.

"Are you seriously asking me for money to feed your fucking habit?" I growl.

His features harden. "I saw the crowd you hang out with."

"What fucking crowd, Jason? Look around you, I'm on my fucking own here!"

"Bullshit," he sneers as he pulls out his phone and taps on the screen then turns it to face me. My breath hitches. It's a photo of me and Corvin from weeks ago, the day he chased me down after coming out of practice. I'm plastered against his front with one of his arms around my waist and the other tangled in my hair, our faces are mere inches apart. "I know he's loaded, I looked him up."

It takes me a few minutes to gather myself and snap out of my stupor, seeing that photo of us has feelings I've been fighting to keep buried begin to resurface. "What?"

He steps into me, forcing me to crane my head back in order to maintain eye contact with him. "My parents cut me off, they froze my trust account. Either you help me or—"

"Or fucking what, Jason? You gonna leak those nude pics of me you took when I was in the shower? You gonna beat me up and force me to give you money?" I'm screaming hysterically now. "Newsflash, asshole, I don't have money and Corvin isn't fucking here. Even if he was, he wouldn't give me shit."

I clamp my mouth closed when his sparks with life. "You been fucking the future quarterback of the Patriots, sweet juice?" I cringe and shake my head rapidly, denying his claim. "Invite me up to your dorm and I promise I won't leak time-stamped pictures of you from when you were sixteen."

"Leak the fucking photos because I'll never invite you up," I spit.

"Invite me up, or I leak them and make it look like he took the photos of you underage." Before I can overthink it and talk myself out of doing it, I knee him right in the balls. "Fuck!" he screams out as he falls to the ground like a sack of shit. I don't waste time as dash across the parking lot and keep running without a destination in sight. All I know is that if I stop running and Jason catches me, I'm as good as dead.

I've been hiding out near Corvin's penthouse, it started raining about an hour ago and I'm drenched. I know if I don't get out of these clothes soon, I'm going to wind up catching a cold. I have two choices, chance going back to my dorm and running into Jason or going to Corvin's penthouse. The thought of Jason getting his hands on me makes the decision easy, Corvin's penthouse it is.

It feels weird being back in this elevator, I have no idea if he even knows that I went to the cabin or that I stayed here when I first got back, and honestly, I hate that he kept his word. He hasn't made contact with me since the day of his first and last game with WFU. Ash was pissed that he bailed on the team, but even he admitted that he would have done exactly what Corvin did if he was given the chance. The doors open and I'm immediately hit with a sense of Deja Vu. I step into the dark, empty place and feel for the light switches on the left hand side of the wall. I turn the lights on and make my way further inside, a part of me wishes he would round the corner but I know that isn't going to happen.

I turn the lights on in the kitchen and place my backpack on the counter. I open it and grab out the playing jersey he left me the last day we were together. I carry this fucking thing everywhere with me and sleep in it. I leave my bag and phone on the counter, then make my way up to his room so I can have a hot shower. I'm chilled to the bone. Stepping into the bathroom, I flick the light on, then reach into the shower and turn it to hot. I walk back into the room and lay the jersey out on the bed before stripping and leaving my wet clothes at the foot of the bed.

I take my time in the shower, washing my hair and using his body lotion. I'll admit I now buy the same body lotion and use it daily. It makes me feel like he's with me and I love how the smell of it reminds me of him.

Fuck, I miss him.

Pain radiates inside my chest, I was a stupid fool. I had him within my grasp. The past six weeks have been torture not being able to see him or speak to him. The only way I know he is alive is because I stalk him on social media. I turn the shower off and step out, grab one of the towels off the rack and wrap it around my body. I grab another towel and use that one to dry my hair. I drop it in the hamper before I step into the room and freeze. A gasp leaves me, my whole body turns to stone at the sight in front of me. Corvin sits on the end of the bed with his head bowed staring down at the playing jersey that I've claimed as my own in his hands. He slowly lifts his head. The moment our gazes collide, I feel something inside me cave and rob me of air. His hair is a tousled mess, a five o'clock shadow now dusts his jawline but it's his eyes, they look hollow and lifeless.

My body begins to heat as his eyes travel over me, his eyes drinking in every exposed inch of my skin. My breathing picks up when I see him clench the jersey in his hold, almost like he needs something to hold onto or risk reaching out for me. The tension between us is so thick that you could cut through it with a knife. I know I need to say something and explain why I'm in his house, but no words will come out of my mouth.

"What are you doing here, Alexa?" *Alexa*, not jail bait. I don't know why the use of my real name from him stings.

"Uh, I…" I take a deep breath and decide to be a grown ass woman. "I came to shower, that's it. Sorry, it won't happen again," I bite out as I close the space between us and snatch the jersey from his hands. I turn ready to head into the bathroom to change and get the fuck out of here, but he has other plans. His hand clamps down on the back of my neck and I'm yanked backward, then pushed down onto the bed while he towers above me. His eyes blaze with anger as he stares down at me.

"Why the fuck are you really here and why do you have that fucking jersey, Alexa?" I grit my teeth and try to focus on his words instead of the fact I'm flat on my back on his bed, with him standing between my legs. Fuck, the sight of him standing there looking all sexy without even trying has me getting wet. "Answer me!" he shouts, snapping me out of my wayward thoughts.

"Jason's here," I blurt out without meaning to, His brows jump to his hairline in surprise. He takes a step back and my stomach sinks thinking he's going to kick me out and tell me to deal with it on my own. It's what I deserve after everything I put him through, but deep down inside, I don't want that. I just want to be near him. I've missed him so fucking much, which is why I leap off the bed and catch him off guard when I wrap my arms around his waist and rest my cheek against his chest. I bask in this moment of having him back, until I hear a woman's voice coming from downstairs.

CHAPTER TWENTY-ONE

Corvin

Coming back to North Carolina was hard. I knew there was a chance I would run into her but what I didn't expect was to come home and find her shit on my counter and her in my shower. The sight of my jersey that I left her on my bed threw me off kilter. I gave that to her for a purpose. The moment I laid eyes on her though, all thoughts fled my mind at the sight of her in nothing but a towel. She stands there looking effortlessly beautiful, her eyes are wide with surprise at the sight of me.

"What are you doing here, Alexa?" I grit out after a minute.

"Uh, I…" She takes a deep breath and steels her spine before she continues. "I came to shower, that's it. Sorry, it won't happen again," she bites out, then closes the space between us and yanks the jersey from my hold. She spins on her heel ready to head for the bathroom, fuck that. I clamp my hand down on the back of her neck and hurl her backward until she lands on the bed staring up at me with wide eyes. Anger thrums through my veins as I scowl down at her, six weeks without seeing her or speaking to her and she thinks she can come into my house and turn her back on me? The girl has lost her fucking mind.

"Why the fuck are you really here and why do you have that fucking jersey, Alexa?" I bite out, needing to know why the fuck she is here. I see her eyes fill with lust and I know without a doubt if I don't get her back on track, I'll wind up giving in and fucking her right here. "Answer me!" I shout.

"Jason's here," she blurts out, surprising the fuck out of me, I never expected her to say that shit. I step back, needing to put some distance between us so I can process her words. I manage one step backward before she's leaping off the bed and throws her arms around my waist and buries her face into my chest. I stand here stiffly, with my arms by my sides, shocked as fuck by her reaction. Kerrie's voice pulls me out of my shock. Alexa tenses against me and I know without a doubt what she is thinking. I refuse to satisfy her and tell her the truth. I want her to stew for a while, she deserves it.

"Corvin, we're going to be late." Alexa slowly untangles her arms from around me and steps back keeping her gaze on the floor.

"Alexa—"

"Don't worry about me," she cuts in. She tries to brush past me but I step in front of her, stopping her from escaping. She finally lifts her gaze to mine, fire burns in the depths of her blue eyes. "Your girlfriend is waiting for you," she spits, and her tone is filled with venom.

"Jealousy looks good on you," I taunt, her nose scrunches up in distaste, she opens her mouth ready to have a go at me until the sound of heels clicking against the stairs draws her attention. She slowly swivels around just as Kerrie reaches the landing. I watch Alexa take her in. Kerrie is beautiful, there is no doubt about that. Blonde, green eyes, tall and has a banging body.

"Oh, sorry. I didn't realize you had… company," Ker says as she looks from Alexa to me.

"Don't worry, *company* was just leaving," Alexa snaps as she shoves past me and storms into the bathroom, slamming the door behind herself. I bite my lip to keep from laughing and shoot Kerrie a knowing look, her eyes widen.

"Is that her?" she mouths. I nod just as the bathroom door opens and Alexa storms out, shoulder checking me on her way past. She stops at the end of the bed and looks down at her wet clothes. A half groan, half growl comes from her before she stomps over to my dresser and yanks open the third drawer, where I store my sweats. Truth is, I'm too focused on the fact she is wearing *my* number on her back and from this angle, I can see the bottom of her ass cheeks peeking out while she's bent over. She slams the drawer, turns around and looks between me and Kerrie with anger plastered all over her face.

"What the hell are you staring at?" Kerrie shakes her head in answer, while I give her a deadpan look.

"You're in *my* room, I live here, remember?" Her face slackens. "I mean, by all means, please help yourself to my clothes," I mock.

"Fuck you, asshole," she snaps as she pulls the sweats on and rolls them a couple times at the waist so they actually fit her. Fuck. The sight of her in my clothes has my cock twitching in my pants, no doubt I'll be rubbing one out to the memory of her wearing my jersey tonight.

"I'll give you two a minute—" Kerrie clamps her mouth shut when Alexa shoots her a scathing look.

"You want to leave your boyfriend alone with me?" Kerrie frowns but Alexa doesn't give her a chance to answer. "You know we've fucked, right?" I choke on air, Kerrie looks like she wants the floor to open up and swallow her whole. "Oh, didn't he tell you about how he fucked my brains out on that bed right there?" she taunts. She saunters toward Kerrie with an evil glint in her eyes, I know without a doubt my vexed little jail bird is about to unleash her fury on my innocent *agent*. I dart forward, wrap my arm around Alexa's waist and lift her. "Put me down asshole!" she screams.

Ignoring her, I look to Kerrie. "Cancel the meeting and reschedule it for tomorrow."

"Will do, I'll call you in the morning," she says with a smile on her face.

"Don't want to stay and fuck your boyfriend?" Alexa taunts. Kerrie scurries down the stairs and the moment I hear the elevator ping to announce Kerrie's exit, I toss the spiteful little shit on the bed and relish in the shriek of surprise that comes from her. I stand over her, crossing my arms over my chest and watch as she scrambles to get off the bed and climb to her feet. Her hair is a wild mess, her eyes shine with malice as she looks at me. "You're a fucking prick!" she seethes.

"And you're a jealous little shit," I snap back.

She scoffs. "Oh, please, I am not jealous. I don't need you. You can fuck who you like and so can I." That's it, my restraint is gone. I strike out and wrap my hand around her throat as I yank her forward and get right in her face.

"If I find out you've fucked anyone while I've been gone, I'll fucking kill them in front of you and fuck you next to them while they bleed out." I sneer right in her face.

"Don't think your high-end hooker of a girlfriend would like that." I dip my head, ghosting my lips over the shell of her ear.

"What pisses you off more, jail bait." She shivers the moment her nickname tumbles from my lips. "The fact Kerrie is beautiful or the fact you think I'm fucking her?" She grips the front of my shirt and pulls me in closer.

"Both," she answers honestly. I draw back and peer down at her. The anger that was present a second ago in her eyes has vanished and is replaced by regret. Her eyes search mine. I wait patiently for her to continue, I refuse to push her again if she wants me then she is going to have to spell it out for me. "I'm pissed off because she is beautiful. No doubt she's closer to your age, which makes being in public with her easier. Does it kill me to know that your face is the last thing she sees before she sleeps and the first thing she sees when she wakes up? Yes. I fucking hate that I missed my chance."

It's a fucking feat to try to remain calm and keep my face blank of emotion… not giveaway the fact her words have me wanting to jump for fucking joy like a toddler, but I won't fall for this shit again, I can't. Being away from her has been hell. I've thrown myself head first into training and prepping to take the field with the Patriots next season. It's the only thing that has been able to keep my mind off her.

"What are you trying to say, Alexa?" I whisper hesitantly. If this is another one of her games, I don't think I would be able to handle that.

She darts her tongue out and moistens her lips. "I could give a million reasons why I'm no good for you." My heart skips a beat in anticipation of her leaving me, again. "But, I have one really good reason why you should pick me and not her." This is the first time I've ever seen her nervous and it's endearing to see.

"Tell me," I push.

Her eyes begin to well with tears, making my breath lodge in my throat. Everything around us seems to fade away as she becomes the center of my orbit and my sole focus. My chest rises and falls rapidly as I wait for her to say the words I've been dreaming about hearing for weeks. She takes a shuddering breath, squares her shoulders and holds my gaze as she speaks. "You should pick me because I'm in love with you." Tears leak from her eyes. "I know I did some fucked up shit to you and I'm sorry. I wanted to wear this jersey to your game but I couldn't until I let go of the past." I frown down at her. "I came to the game and watched you from a distance. I wanted to run to you when it was over, but I knew if I wanted to make this work with you, I needed to let go of Cody."

"What does that mean?" I ask.

"I flew back to visit Cody and your... house." My eyes widen.

"You went back to the house at CHU?" She nods. "Why?"

"I needed to see for myself that you did nothing wrong, I know you didn't but I just had to see it and have no doubts. Katie told me what you did for Cody. I had no right to treat you the way I did, Corvin. I was an utter bitch and you still bailed me out and gave me a place to stay. I'm sorry I wasn't in the seat at the game. I should have been and I'll regret that forever but please, tell me I'm not too late."

"Too late for what?"

Her face scrunched in pain. "Too late to tell you that I love you and want to be with you." I clasp her face between my hands and use my thumbs to brush away her tears.

"Do you mean it?" She opens her mouth, but I push on, "I need you to be sure, Alexa, because if we do this, I'm all in. I'm a possessive son of a bitch and I don't share, baby, not even with my boys."

"What about the *THOT*?" she grits out and I laugh. She glares at me.

"Did you really just call my *agent* a hoe?" Embarrassment clouds her features, her mouth hangs open and I grin. "Yeah, baby, *that hoe over there* is my agent, not my girlfriend." If I wasn't afraid that she would rip my dick off, I'd snap a pic of her face right now. It's a mix between shame, guilt and victory.

She shrugs her shoulders, trying to act cool but we both know she just got knocked down a peg. "Well, what did you expect me to think, Reaper?"

I purse my lips and decide to be honest about something before I put her out of her misery. "Since you now know I had nothing to do with Cody's death, can we maybe stop with the

Reaper name?" The moment she frowns and scrunches her face up, I tense knowing this is about to cause a fight. I open my mouth ready to backpedal until she pushes my sweats down her legs and kicks them to the side, while never breaking eye contact with me.

CHAPTER TWENTY-TWO

Alexa

I love the way his eyes spark with need. I slowly back up until the backs of my knees hit the bed. "At the start, I called you Reaper for obvious reasons but as time went on, the meaning behind the name changed." He takes a step toward me, then pauses as he grips the hem of his shirt and yanks it over his head tossing it to the side. I drink in the sight of his chiseled body and fight the moan from breaking free—fuck, his body is a work of art. He comes at me but stops, keeping an inch of space between us.

"Changed to what?"

It takes me a second to remember what we were talking about thanks to the distraction of his perfectness on display. "I now call you Reaper because you killed any chance of me not loving you." His eyes widen at my declaration. "I'm gonna say this one last time, Reaper, I love you and want you but the question is, do you feel the same way?"

The words are barely out of my mouth before he's on me, crashing his lips against mine. I open for him and moan the moment the taste of him hits my senses. I wrap my arms around his neck as he slides his hand between our bodies and cups my pussy. I gasp and break the kiss.

"This is mine," he growls as he slips a finger inside my tight wet hole, forcing a cry from me. "Your age means nothing to me, jail bait. You're legal. If anyone has a problem with us, then I'll take care of it. I love you, Alexa," he says as he continues to work his finger in and out of me, making it near impossible to focus on anything he just said. He leans down and places open-mouthed kisses on my neck. I grip his arms for support as I open my legs wider, giving him better access to finger fuck me. "You let anyone else touch my pussy, jail bait?" he growls before biting my neck and sucking the flesh into his mouth.

"Fuck!" I cry out. He releases my neck and draws back to meet my gaze as he lazily fingers my cunt.

"Answer me." Corvin is kind, loving and sweet on the daily, but the moment you get him in the bedroom it's like a switch flicks. He becomes this dominant ultra-possessive beast that you want to obey without thought.

"No. No one touched me."

He smiles approvingly. "Good girl." I moan, hearing those two words from him always gets me wet. He pulls his finger out and I whimper. I watch as he brings that finger to his mouth and sucks it clean, moaning at the taste. My mouth parts slightly. "Hmm, you taste good baby." I swallow audibly too transfixed on the sight of him sucking my juices off his finger to respond. "Get on the bed and open your legs, I want to look at my pussy."

Fuck, his words have my clit throbbing with need. I do as he says and climb on the bed. Rolling over, I rest back against the pillows, bend my legs at the knees and part them. I keep my eyes on him as I watch his reaction. His eyes darken immediately at the sight, his gaze remaining on my pussy as he reaches down and pops the button on his jeans, then yanks the zipper down. He pushes his jeans and boxers down in one swift motion, his cock springing free and slapping against his stomach. The sight of his hard dick has my mouth watering for a taste. He leans forward, wraps his arms around my thighs and buries his face in my pussy.

"Fuck," I scream out and arch off the bed, there is no work up or playing around. His tongue pushes inside my wet hole as he brings his hand over the top of my thigh and presses his thumb against my clit. It's been weeks since I've come, so I know I won't last much longer at this pace. He isn't coaxing an orgasm from me, he's forcing it out of me and I'm slightly terrified of the feelings swirling inside me. I feel like it will rip me apart. "Corvin, it's too much," I plead. He keeps circling my clit with his thumb as he draws his face back and stares up at me.

"Come all over my fucking face now or you don't get to come at all tonight." Before a protest can formulate, he buries his face in my pussy. There isn't a thing I can do except trust him to hold me together, as I tear apart from the orgasm he is ripping out of me. The moment I come, I scream his name, so loud people on the floor below us would be able to hear. I feel like a tidal wave has ripped its way through my body. My vision blurs and my limbs lock up as the most intense orgasm I have experienced courses through my body. Corvin brings me down slowly, knowing that I need to be eased down or risk passing out. As the final aftershock leaves me, he crawls up my limp body and smashes his lips against mine. He shoves his tongue inside my mouth, wanting me to taste my own release and I'll admit, it's the hottest fucking thing ever, sucking my cum off his tongue. He breaks the kiss and smirks sexily down at me. "Good girl."

Fuck, I just realized I have a praise kink and judging from the look in his eyes, he already picked up on that fact. He reaches between our bodies and lines his cock up with my entrance. I open my legs as wide as I can to accommodate him better, but the man is double my size so it's a bit hard. The moment I feel the head of his cock prodding at my entrance and a wave of heat runs through me. He holds my gaze as he slowly pushes inside me. This moment, right here, is so intense. Yes, his cock slowly inching side of me is part of the reason, but majority of the reason is because we both have no walls up. He is letting me see the love he feels for me and I'm showing him without words that I'm madly in love with him. This is a moment I'll never forget.

We both moan loudly the second he is balls deep inside me. "I love you, Alexa." His declaration shocks me. A watery smile spreads across my face as I reach up, cup his cheeks and place a tender kiss to his lips before pulling back.

"I love you too." A cocky look enters his gaze.

"I know." I snort out a laugh that quickly morphs in a moan as he thrusts inside me. Unlike last time, he doesn't go slow and make love to me. He fucks me like a starved man who is claiming his woman. "Fuck yes, baby," he growls when I lock my legs around his waist to draw him inside me deeper, but I need more.

"Get on your back and let me fuck you." It's almost comical at how quickly he flips us and allows me to take the lead. I reach down to take his jersey off but he grips my hands, halting my movements.

"Leave it on. I wanna fuck my girl with my number on her back." Hearing him call me his girl has butterflies taking flight in my belly. I place my hands flat on his chest as I bend my knees. I'm in a squatting position now and I know he won't last long this way and nor will I, but I need to feel his cum inside me. I start to bounce up and down on his cock and relish in the way his eyes widen and groans continuously come from him. "Fuck, baby, just like that," he grits out as he reaches down and uses the pad of his thumb to apply pressure to my clit. Fuck. I throw my head and cry out my release as I come all over his cock. He wraps his arms around my waist and holds me in place as he takes over and thrusts inside me chasing his own release. "Alexa!" Hearing him shout my name as he comes apart beneath me has a sick sense of satisfaction thrumming through me.

I flop forward and bury my face in the crook of his neck, the only sounds that can be heard are our ragged breaths. His arms band around me as he rolls us onto our sides so we are facing each other, then slowly pulls out of me. I clamp my thighs closed so his cum doesn't leak out on the bedspread. I may be young but even I know having cum stains on your sheets isn't a good look. He reaches up and cups my cheek. His eyes drill into mine and I see everything he feels for me, robbing me of my breath.

"I never expected to come back here tonight and find you." I smile shyly.

"It wasn't supposed to happen, but I'm not mad that it did." He grins at my answer.

"I'm not mad at all. Have you been staying here?" He doesn't sound mad, just genuinely curious.

"I did after I got back from Easter break, hoping you would come back here after training camp."

He frowns. "How did you know I was at training camp?" Oh shit, I nibble on my bottom lip nervously. "My cum is inside you right now and you're being shy over telling me how you knew where I was?" I snort out a laugh and he chuckles.

"I went to your cabin over Easter break to win you back." His eyes widen.

"You… what?" Confusion is clear in his tone, so I explain further.

"I managed to convince Katie and Nathan to take me to your cabin after I saw Cody. I thought you would be there, but you weren't and I got to deal with your amazing sister." He bites down on his bottom lip to keep from laughing. I roll my eyes.

"Leah's a real peach, isn't she?" I snort.

"I see why you had no say in her dating your best friend."

He laughs and nods. "Seriously though, your sister loves you and she had every right to say what she did. All your friends love you and that's really cool."

"Wait, so weeks ago you had planned to tell me you loved me?" I nod. "Why didn't you call me?"

"Uh, because when Darius and the others tried to call, you didn't answer and then text saying you couldn't have your phone on you."

He scowls over at me giving me pause, what the hell did I do? "You're different! If you had of called, I would have answered."

My heart soars, he has no idea how much that fucking means to me. I place a chaste kiss to his lips. He wraps an arm around my waist and hurls me back on top of him, holding me against his chest. "Well, I didn't know that then. After I left them, I came back here hoping you would show up. After two weeks, I gave up and went back to my dorm. It became too hard to be here without you." His face slackens, then he reaches up and runs his fingers through my hair, grips the back of my head and pulls me down until my lips are meshed against his. Before I can deepen the kiss I pull back and cringe. "I need to shower."

He frowns. "What?" Shaking my head I push off him and stand at the edge of the bed, drinking in the sight of him naked and *he's mine*. "My eyes are up here, baby." I tear my gaze from his cock and shoot him a filthy look.

"I have your cum dripping down my thighs—"

"Don't give a fuck. Get your ass back in this bed now, Alexa. You're going to be covered in my cum from head to toe by the time the sunrises." My brows jump to my hairline. I must not move fast enough for him, in the next second he slips off the bed, stands in front of me and growls out. "Get on your knees like a good girl."

Jesus Christ, I'm so fucking in love with this man.

CHAPTER TWENTY-THREE

Corvin

Alexa stirs beside me and I groan as I tighten my hold around her waist and draw her naked ass into me, then bury my face in her hair. A small chuckle escapes her as she rolls over in my hold and faces me. It takes me a second to gather the courage to open my eyes.

"Open your eyes," she demands quietly.

"Nope."

"Why not?"

"What if this was all a dream and the moment I open my eyes, you'll vanish and I'll be back to being heartbroken." I feel her melt into me, then in the next second her lips are pressed against mine, her tongue prods at my lips, forcing her way inside. I growl and flip us so I'm on top of her. She laughs, breaking the kiss and I finally open my eyes.

"Hi." I melt into her.

"Hello, beautiful." I use my knees to push her legs open wider. Her eyes darken and her breathing kicks up notch, knowing she's about to be fucked senseless. Even though we only managed to get an hour or two of sleep. thanks to us not being able to keep our hands off each other, it's not enough and I need more. "You wet for me, baby?"

"Always," She replies huskily. I'm lining my cock up with her entrance, ready to fuck her brains out, but freeze the moment I hear the *ding* announcing the elevators arrival. I groan and flop forward growling into her neck. "You've got to be kidding me. This is the fucking second time this shit has happened." Laughter bubbles out of me.

"Corvin!" My laughter dies in my throat at the sound of the panic in Kerrie's voice. I push up and place a quick kiss on her lips before I get my ass out of bed. "Corvin?" I shoot Alexa an apologetic look. She rolls her eyes playfully.

"Coming, woman, hold the fuck on!" I shout. As I find the sweats Alexa was wearing last night and pull them on, I look back at my girl. Fuck, she looks incredible—naked, hair wild and that hungry look in her eyes has me cursing Kerrie's fucking timing. "Meet me downstairs."

"I'm gonna shower, I need to get to class." My stomach sinks.

"Can you skip?" She narrows her eyes.

"There is only two weeks left. I need to be there but you can drive me?" I smile wide and nod like an idiot.

"Deal, baby." I rush down the stairs to find a red-faced Kerrie standing at the counter with a don't fuck with me look on her face. "What's up?"

Her nostrils flare. "Who the fuck is the girl upstairs, Corvin?" I tense and pin her with a look that dares her to fuck with me.

"She's my girlfriend. If you want to keep your fucking job, you'll watch how you speak about her." She doesn't seem fazed by the venom that laces each of my words. I won't have Kerrie coming here and trying to ruin what I have. I just got my girl and like fuck will I let some bitch come into my house and speak about her like that.

"How old is she?" she grits out. I school my features.

"Seventeen."

"Jesus Christ." She sneers and tosses me her phone. I catch it and shoot her a questioning look. "Read it." I open the phone and immediately my stomach churns. There are pictures of Alexa naked in a shower but her tits and ass are blurred. The headline reads *Patriots new QB likes em young*.

"I… Who the fuck did this?" I breath out as I look to Kerrie.

"I have no idea but the photos are date and time stamped, Corvin. She was sixteen at the time of these photos." I shake my head.

"I never slept with her until she was seventeen. I've done nothing wrong. I haven't broken any laws here, Kerrie, she is legal."

She throws her hands in the air. "She's technically still a fucking minor." I flinch.

"How do we fix this?" She blows out a breath and runs a hand through her hair as she tries to come up with a way to spin this story in our favor. The longer she remains silent and continues to pace the floor in front of me, I begin to worry.

"How attached would you say you are?" I glare at her.

"Alexa isn't going anywhere," I snarl. She rolls her eyes and resumes her pacing as I stand here praying that this wasn't something she did to fuck with me. I hear her coming down the stairs and spin around. She's wearing one of my shirts and another pair of my sweats. She pauses a few feet away from me and looks to Kerrie then back to me.

"What's going on?" The hesitancy in her voice and the confused look on her face has me hoping that it wasn't her that sold these photos to the press. Not only would this fuck up my career, it would also fuck with BCD'S and I can't have that.

"Alexa, right?" Kerrie says in a tone filled with authority. Alexa looks to her and sizes her up before dismissing her and looking back to me.

"What's going on, Corvin?" I take a deep breath before telling her.

"Someone sold pictures of you to the press." She scrunches her face in confusion. "Nude photos of you at the age of sixteen." A natural reaction would be to scream, cry or even look shocked but she shows neither of those emotions and my heart drops. "You knew about the pictures," I whisper.

"Yes." I stumble backward and have to grip the counter to stop myself from falling to my ass.

"You sold the pictures?" Kerrie accuses. Alexa ignores her and keeps her gaze fixed on me. She searches my face for a second and a look of hurt flashes through her eyes before she masks it just as quickly.

"You think I sold the pictures to get back at you?" She doesn't give me a chance to answer. "Fuck you. I told you I loved you and let you in. I fucking let you in, Corvin, and I've never let anyone in." She's shouting now but I'm unable to say a single word. "I never sold the fucking picture, you prick!" she screams before she barges past Kerrie, swipes her phone and bag off the counter and storms toward the elevators. The sight of her walking away from me and out of my life again, snaps me out of my stupor and I chase after her.

"Alexa, wait," I shout as I round the corner but I'm too late, the doors are already closing and the last thing I see are tears trailing down her cheeks and the look of utter devastation in her eyes that will haunt me. "Fuck," I roar. I'm not losing her again. I saw it in her eyes, she didn't do this. I march back into the kitchen and look to Kerrie. "She didn't do it."

"Corvin, she knew about the photos." I grit my teeth.

"She didn't do this," I shout. Kerrie flinches and backs up a step. "I have to go find her," I say as I race up the stairs and grab my phone off the side table. I scroll through my contacts and click on her number, I hit dial.

It rings four times before she answers. "Corvin?"

I sigh in relief. "Katie, I need your help."

After enlisting the help of Katie to get all the sites with the pictures shut down, I send Kerrie on her way to do damage control as I go after my girl. I hop behind the wheel of my Cielo Spyder and plant my foot. I fucked up this morning and I know she isn't going to forgive me easily for doubting her. Clearly she isn't the only one who has to let go of the past. I scan the streets hoping to catch her if she decided to walk instead of catching an Uber, but no such luck. I pull into the parking lot of her dorm building and double park not giving a shit if my car gets towed.

I run across the lot and race up the stairs, yanking on the door but the fucker is locked and I don't have a card to get in. Last time I was lucky and came in the same time as another girl was leaving. I pull my phone out of my pocket and call her, it goes straight to voicemail.

"Shit!" I check the time on my phone and decide to try the workshop. I run back to my car and drive to the other side of campus. I park legally this time and run across the quad toward the workshop, in the east wing. Students gawk at me and I see a few of them pull them their phones out—fucking idiots think videoing me running around will get them views on Instagram. I slam to a stop in front of the classroom door and pray she is here. The moment I open the door a relieved sigh escapes me, she sits in the back of the room with her head down and her phone clasped between her hands. When she hears the door click shut behind me, she snaps her head up, confusion at the sight of me is clear in her features.

"What the hell are you doing here?" Anger laces each of her words and I honestly can't blame her, I should never have doubted her. I make my way toward her and watch her grow tenser the closer I get. I take it as a win that she doesn't throw the tools on the desk in front of her at me. I stop beside her desk and look down at her.

"I'm here for you, jail bait." She scoffs.

"How fitting is that name now, huh?" I cringe.

"I never should have doubted you, Alexa. I was an idiot for ever thinking you would do that but I won't lie, a small part of me did wonder if you were playing me."

She sighs and her shoulders slump. "I told you last night that I was sorry for everything I did to you. I fucking told you I loved you, Corvin, and I've never told anyone that before." Guilt wars inside me. I reach out and grip her face between my hands and rest my forehead against hers. Neither of us say a word for a moment as we just breathe each other in and relish the feeling of being together.

"I'm sorry, jail bait."

"I didn't do it, Corvin." I see it in her eyes, she may not have done it but she knows who did.

"Who did it?"

She inhales unsteadily. "Jason threatened to post the pictures if I didn't give him money. I thought he was bluffing. I swear if I knew he was actually serious I would have paid the fucking money to save you this trouble." Anger courses through me, I forgot all about that son of bitch and her telling me he was here.

"Where is he?" I snarl.

"I have no idea, he just pops up randomly."

"How did he know you were here?" I ask hesitantly, slightly worried that she was the one who told him.

"He tracked my phone," she whispers. I remain silent for a minute as I try to formulate a plan.

"What classes does he have?" She shakes her head.

"He isn't a student here. He said he was taking a gap year. His parents cut him off and now he's broke and can't feed his habit. He saw a picture of me and you on one of your fan pages." The jealousy I detect in her tone has me fighting back a smile. "He thought seeing that picture meant I was loaded."

I place a kiss to her lips and try to smile reassuringly. "It's okay, baby. I have to do something but I'll be waiting for you after school."

"What are you going to do?"

"I'm going to make your ex wish his mother swallowed."

CHAPTER TWENTY-FOUR

Alexa

I'm on edge all freaking day. My phone is dead, so I haven't been able to contact Corvin at all to find out what he's been up to. The moment the professor says we can leave, I'm out of my seat and racing out the front of the building, ready to head back to my dorm, charge my phone and call Corvin. I push through the doors, only to be greeted by a crowd of students. I push through them and try to get the hell out of here but an arm snakes out, grips my wrist and yanks me sideways. I spin around ready to punch whoever the fuck it is for laying hands on me, until I look up and see Corvin.

I look around and now the crowd makes sense, they're all gathered around to catch a glimpse of the Patriots future QB. "So humble," I mutter as he smiles for a picture. He throws his head back and laughs, then slings his arm around my shoulders and walks us away from the crowd of thirsty students. It grates on my nerves to see girls flaunt what their mama gave them in front of Corvin. I look up at him to see if he is checking them out, but I'm pleasantly surprised to see his gaze is fixed on me.

"All I see is you, baby." Well shit, now I'm all warm and fuzzy inside. He walks us out to the parking lot and opens the passenger door for me. Once I'm secured inside, he races around to his side, starts the car and peels out of the lot. Only then am I able to breathe easier. I couldn't handle having that many people flocking to my feet every day. He drives across campus toward my dorm. After parking, we both climb out and walk hand in hand inside. I admit, it feels kinda nice to not have any reservations about him anymore and just enjoy the fact that he's my boyfriend. Gah, that is gonna take a minute to get used to saying.

We reach my floor and I fish my key out of my pocket, then step inside my mess of a room. Corvin doesn't say a word about the state of my room but his facials practically scream his distaste at the mess.

"I've had exams and don't have time to clean between school and studying," I defend. He raises his hands in surrender.

"I didn't say a word."

"Your face said it for you," I huff, then he chuckles and wraps his arms around me, pulling me in close. I melt into him instantly.

"I missed you."

I smile. "I missed you too." He rests his chin atop my head and tightens his hold on me.

"I'm sorry about this morning, baby. I swear that will never happen again, you have my word." Call me crazy but I believe him. He tells me to pack a bag for a few nights. I don't fight him on it because the truth is, I want to spend as much time with him as I can before he has to go back to New England. After packing a bag with clothes, I start to gather all the text books and anything else I'll need, apparently I won't be coming back to my dorm until next week. It's cool though. I only have two classes tomorrow and then it's the weekend. Next week I have my final two exams, one on Tuesday and the other on Wednesday, then I'm off for the summer!

Corvin helps me carry my bags to the car, laughter

bubbles out of me at the stupid joke he cracked. "Sweet juice." My laughter cuts off as I slowly turn away from Corvin to see Jason standing there with a shit eating grin on his face. I feel Corvin press against my back. He grips my hips possessively, showing Jason that I'm his. "I was right. You are fucking the rich prick."

I snort readying to have a go at the self-righteous prick but Corvin beats me to it. "She sure is, my friend." Corvin may seem calm but I can hear the undercurrent of rage in his tone. "Now, if you'll excuse us, we have plans that require a closed door and no clothing." I nearly choke on my spit. Jason's face is a picture of rage and I know without a doubt he isn't going to let this little moment go any time soon. Corvin ushers me over to the car, opens my door and pushes me inside before joining me on the driver's side. I watch Jason slowly disappear in the side mirror. The moment I can no longer see him, I breathe easier.

Corvin helps me carry my bags from the car to the elevator, there's tension between us thanks to Jason and I hate it. I decide to talk to him about it once we get inside. The doors open and immediately I smile, coming back here feels like home. I go ahead of Corv and pay no attention to my surroundings. As I round the corner, I scream bloody fucking murder the moment Leah jumps out at me. I swear it's a reflex, I don't mean to do it, but she scared me, and my knee-jerk reaction was to throw the two bags in my hands at her.

"Fucking hell, Lee," Corvin reprimands from behind me. I rush forward and inspect her for injury. She purses her lips to the side and gives me a disapproving look.

"Was that fucking necessary?" she snaps. I stare at her like she has lost her mind.

"Dude, you literally hid around a corner and jumped out

at me. How the fuck was I supposed to know you weren't a killer or something hiding in my boyfriend's house?" The moment her jaw unhinges and I hear someone coughing behind her, I know I just fucked up. I peer over her shoulder to see Darius choking on a glass of water. I bite my lip nervously, worried that Corvin will be mad I said something, but honestly it just slipped out. All the worry evaporates inside me the moment he comes up behind me and wraps an arm around my waist. Leah looks from her brother to me, shock evident in her gaze.

"Well, about fucking time. At least now he won't have to keep buying cars and furnishing his house." I cringe in Corvin's hold as he growls from behind me.

"Shut up, asshole, if I recall, my sister fucked with you as well." Leah throws her head back and groans as Darius comes to stand beside her.

"Oh yes, she does." I feel Corvin shudder and laugh, his hold on me tightens.

"Who's side are you on, jail bait?" he snaps but his words lack heat. I pat the hand he has wrapped around me and tilt my head back to look up at him.

"Yours, duh." He smirks triumphantly.

"Eww!" I dart my gaze toward Leah and frown at the disgusted look on her face.

"What?" I ask.

"You were making fuck me eyes at my brother and I don't like it." Both Corvin and Darius snort out a laugh, then gather my bags and take them upstairs for me while Leah and I head into the living room to catch up. The boys come back down and disappear down the hallway toward Corvin's office. The moment we hear the door shut, Leah shifts along the sofa and gets as close as she can to me. "I want every detail. Tell me everything and don't leave a single thing out. Don't deny me, Alexa, I need all the ammo I can get."

"Why?" I ask hesitantly.

She sighs dramatically. "He always throws me fucking his best friend in my face, so I need details, dirt or anything… just hurry and spill before they come back!" I do as she says and fill her in on how Corvin and I reconnected. I refused to tell her about us having sex even when asked. There is no way she is using my sex life as ammo for their next fight. I even fill her in on the events of this morning and running into Jason before we arrived back here. "What the fuck?" she shouts. I try to shush her but it's too late, I hear the guys running toward us. They burst into the living room looking like they are ready to break up a fight.

"What'd you do?" Corvin shouts as he pins Leah with a dirty look. She takes it in stride and slowly climbs to her feet. I follow her lead and keep both of them in my line of sight as I take a few steps back. I feel Darius brush up beside me and whisper.

"Whatever happens, stay out of it." I nod my understanding. I've had plenty of fights with sisters and know to keep my nose out of sibling drama.

"I didn't do shit, exactly like you didn't do shit when her ex-boyfriend posted fucking nudes of her online!" she screams. Corvin darts his gaze to me and I look down feeling shitty. I don't expect him to take care of all my problems and I'm annoyed that Leah is throwing me under the bus right now.

"I'm handling it!" he grits out. That garners my attention, I look at him in surprise.

"You are?" I question and ignore Darius's sigh from beside me.

His shoulders deflate. "Of course I am. He fucking posted nudes of you online, Alexa. I'm not gonna let that shit go. Darius is here to help me. Beckett, Saint and Crue will arrive later tonight as well."

"We are?"

"They are?" Leah and I both say in unison.

Corvin takes a calming breath before coming over to me and cupping my face in his large hands. "Yes, they are here to help take down your bitch of an ex. I plan to ruin that fucking piece of scum and make sure his life isn't worth living after what he did to you." I see it in his eyes, he isn't lying and he means everything he says. Before I can utter a word Leah cuts in and asks.

"If Becky is coming, does that mean Val is too?" Corvin takes a deep breath and nods stiffly. I reach out and grip his waist in my hands offering him my silent support.

"Yeah, Valance and Dawson are coming as well." Katie told me about the situation between him and Val, like me, he needed someone to blame and I understand exactly how he is feeling right now.

"Are you going to be okay with her being here?" I ask quietly. He mulls over my words for a beat before answering.

"As long as you're with me, I'll be fine." I fucking swoon like a love-sick little girl. He leans down and covers my mouth with his, the moment his tongue slips inside my mouth a whimper of need escapes me.

"Oh, fuck this! That is wrong and gross." Corvin breaks our kiss and shoots me a wink before turning to face his sister, who looks thoroughly repulsed.

"What is it you used to say to me, *if you don't like it look away then*." Her eyes widen and I bite my lip to keep from laughing at him mocking her.

"I don't sound like that and for the record, when you hear me screaming your best friend's name tonight remember this moment."

"Fuck, Goldie!" Corvin ignores Darius's protest and smiles wide at his sister.

"Of course, Lee, but it may be hard hearing you scream his name because Alexa will be screaming *mine* louder."

Oh, for the love of God, this is just wrong. How am I turned on at the thought of seeing who can make which girl scream louder?

CHAPTER TWENTY-FIVE

Corvin

"By the looks of things Katie was able to remove the pictures from every site on the web." I sigh in relief at Darius's words. "Who is this guy?" I look up from my computer and stare at Darius across my desk. After mine and Leah's little show-down, we retreated to my office to do damage control. Thankfully I think with the help of Katie, we were able to scrub this story out before it reached the managing staff of the Patriots, a scandal like this would have ended my chances of playing for them.

"He's her ex and he showed up here a week after she returned from break…" I fill him in on all the details. I also tell him about their relationship and how he used to use his fists to solve his problems.

Anger brims in his eyes, he's ridged and grinding his teeth so fucking hard I fear he may break them. "He fucking goes down, tonight," he grits out through clenched teeth.

I smile darkly at my best friend. "As soon as we finish dinner with Troy and the others, we go after him."

"You know where he is?"

Shaking my head, I lift my hand and show him the message thread. "I stole his number from Alexa's phone and promised to pay the cunt whatever he wanted if he deleted the photos and disappeared from her life."

Darius smiles wider than the Cheshire cat. "How much does he think he's getting?"

"Two million." He whistles between his teeth and then cracks his neck side to side.

"I'm fucking pumped, it's been too long since we fucked some deserving prick up." I look him directly in the eyes so he can see I'm fucking serious when I speak.

"We do not kill him. We can fuck him up and break some bones, but I'm not dealing with another death, I can't," I say in a firm tone letting him know I'm not fucking budging on this.

After leaving Darius downstairs to get ready for dinner, I head up to my room. Thank fuck I got the downstairs shower fixed. Once I reach the landing, I look around for my girl but she's nowhere in sight. I make my way over to the bathroom and push the door open. My mouth hangs open at the sight of her naked and stepping out of the shower, water droplets trailing down her perfect body. She grabs a towel from the shelf and wraps it around her body, then steps in front of the mirror. Fuck this. I close the door behind me and plaster myself against her back. She meets my gaze in the mirror looking slightly unsure of what I'm doing.

"You okay?" she asks.

"Be a good girl and drop the towel." Her eyes darken. I hold her gaze in the mirror as I rid myself of my shirt and drop my pants, kicking them to the side before resuming my spot behind her. She gasps when she feels my hard cock against her back. "Lose the fucking towel," I snap. She swallows and nods robotically. With shaky hands, she reaches up and releases the knot in the towel. I waste no time, reaching around I cup both her tits in my hands and tweak her nipples. Her head lulls back against my chest as a moan slips free. I continue to twirl her nipple in my left hand and glide my right hand down her stomach until I reach her pussy. She gasps the moment I cup her. "You wet for me, baby?"

She lazily lifts her head and meets my gaze in the mirror. "Yes," she breathes out as I slip a finger between her folds and circle her clit a couple times before finally reaching further down.

"Fuck," I groan the moment I feel how slick she is. I push my finger inside her slowly, loving the way she melts into me. I pull my finger free and bring it up to her lips. Her eyes meet mine in the mirror, her pupils are blown wide. "Suck it." She opens her mouth and wraps her sinful lips around my digit and sucks it clean, making my cock twitch against her back. Pulling my finger free, I grip her right leg and lift it, placing it on the edge of the counter. "Leave it there," I bark as I grip my cock and line it up with her entrance. "Hold on, this is going to be hard and fast." She leans forward and grips the edge of the basin, then meets my gaze in the mirror right as I slam inside her.

"Fuck," she screams. I clamp my hand over her mouth to keep her quiet. Contrary to what I said earlier, I have no intention of letting my sister or my best friend hear my girl come. I'm the only one who gets to hear the sounds she makes.

"Look at how beautiful you look with my cock inside you," I rasp out as I continue to pound inside her tight wet cunt. She flicks her gaze and watches my cock ramming in and out of her. A shudder rolls through her. "You like me fucking you like this, don't you, baby?" She moans into my hand. I reach around her front with my free hand and pinch her clit between my fingers. She pushes up onto her tiptoes and screams into my hand. I feel the walls of her pussy starting to clamp down on my cock. I hold her gaze in the mirror and love the blissed-out look in her eyes. "Come on my cock like a good girl." My words are her undoing. Her pussy strangles the life out of my cock as she pushes her back against my chest and screams into my hand as shudders roll through her. I slam inside her twice more before I bite on the soft flesh between her neck and shoulder to mute the sounds coming from me as I come inside the most perfect pussy.

The four of us arrive at the restaurant where we are meeting the others half an hour late. I have fucking needs and sue me, I needed to bust a nut and my girl was down so I had no choice. Well, that's the story I'm going with and if any of them have a problem, they can kiss my ass.

"I can't even look at you, how could you let him defile you." I hide my laughter behind a cough. Leah shoots me a scathing look. Apparently, my hand didn't do shit to mute the sounds coming from my girl, the moment we made it downstairs the look on my sister's face told me they heard everything. Alexa snorts and huddles into my side. I wrap my arm around her as we begin walking toward the entrance of the restaurant. Darius slings his arm around Leah's shoulder and pulls her in close. Seeing how much he loves her makes seeing them together easier.

"Did you give my sister shit for fucking him as well, or am I just lucky?" I tense, Darius's eyes widen but Leah, she just scrunches her face up as she thinks on it for a minute before shaking her head.

"I guess you're just lucky." Darius and I are tense as fuck as we wait for the two of them to argue but clearly mentioning Cody isn't a taboo subject for them. "Plus, Cody and him weren't like how you two are, so it's easy to rile him up now." Both of the girls laugh, while I'm fucking stumped and have no idea what happened just now.

We follow the waiter as he leads us to the back of the swanky restaurant Saint chose. I've never been here before and honestly, the looks the other patrons shoot us tells me it's one of those bougie places where money talks and bullshit walks. We round a corner and then I spot them. Beck stands from his seat the moment my sister breaks away from D and runs toward him. She flings herself at him, he catches her with a loving smile on his face. I don't get their dynamic or what the fuck happened between them to make them as close as they are, but I know without a doubt that Beckett would do anything for my sister. Darius better hope he doesn't fuck with her because it won't just be me hunting him down now.

"Becky, I missed you!" Leah whines as he places her back on her feet, the loving look in his eyes stumps me. Beck was so closed off and unreadable but since Leah came back, she seems to have brought a whole other side of him out and I know he's more open and talkative now because of... Val. I look past Beck and the guys to find Val sitting at the furthest end of the table with Dawson in the seat beside her. Her gaze is focused on the plate in front of her. She must feel my gaze on her, as she slowly lifts her head and our eyes lock. I pull away from Alexa and make my way around to the table toward her. The others stop talking as they all watch, I can feel Beckett's stare drilling holes into the side of my head. If I hurt his baby momma, he and I will be throwing hands. Val slowly rises to her feet as I get closer, and clasps her hands in front of her awkwardly. I keep a foot of space between us. I see the guilt in her eyes and it fucking pains me to know I'm the reason she has been feeling this way for so long.

We stand here for a minute silently just looking at each other, the tension that was present a few seconds ago slowly starts to disappear. Tears begin to build in her eyes, her bottom lip trembles. "I'm so sorry—"

"Fuck," I grit out, cutting her off as I wrap my arms around her tiny frame and pull her against me. She wraps her arms around my waist and buries her face in my chest as she cries. I hold her close, resting my cheek against her head just breathing her in. "I had no right, no fucking right at all to place any blame on you, Val," I whisper low enough for only her to hear. She pulls back, but grips the front of my shirt as I cup her face and wipe away her tears with my thumbs.

"You had every right." I shake my head but she pushes on, "I deserved it." Bending down so we are at eye level, I get right in her face.

"No. What happened to Cody was a horrible freak accident. You never asked for that sick bastard to come after you. We knew there was a risk and if I had of answered that call, she might have been with us still." Guilt laces each of my words, I know the guilt I feel about not taking her call will stay with me for the rest of my life and I'm slowly coming to terms with that. "I'm so sorry for how I've treated you. You have every right to hate me and never speak to me again—"

Val cuts me off. "I could never hate you, Corv." Hearing that from her has a relieved sigh escaping me.

"If it helps." Val and I both turn to face Alexa. "I smashed his car up and burnt it, then got arrested and called him to bail me out." Saint and Crue snicker from their seats, while Beck tries to mask his laughter but fails. Darius and Leah both look anywhere but at me. I narrow my eyes at my girlfriend.

"You also trashed my house," I add. She rolls her eyes and waves her hand in the air, brushing me off.

"Well, let's not dwell on the past, eh?" Everyone begins to laugh at my expense and I'm not even mad about it. Alexa's little joke broke the tension and I'm fucking grateful for that. We all claim our seats. I look around the table at my brothers, my sister, my nephew, Val and my girl, then smile. A few months ago I never thought I would smile again or feel happiness, but right here, right now, I can actually say I am happy!

CHAPTER TWENTY-SIX

Alexa

Sitting around this table with everyone and conversing with each of them easily is so strange. I've never felt like I belonged anywhere before, even with Cody. She was my sister and I always felt like a burden on her. She was always there for me whenever I needed her but I always felt like I was keeping her from her life. Even after Jason and I split, I went to CHU and she never said it but I knew me being there was a nuisance for her. That was her place and her friends and I didn't belong but now, I feel like I finally found my place.

"Where's Katie?" At the mention of Katie's name, I focus back on the conversation around me, Saint and Crue both clamp their mouths closed and drop their gazes to their laps at Val's question. Val looks around the table at each of us and I make sure to avoid looking at her, the shit Katie told me isn't my news to share.

"Well, that was one way to make shit awkward," Corvin chimes in. Awkward laughter sounds out around the table but Saint and Crue still refuse to speak. I debate on whether I should say something or not, when I think back to everything Katie has done for me, I sigh knowing I have to say something.

"You both need to call her before it's too late." They both snap their heads toward me. I keep my face free of emotion, Crue's eyes narrow.

"She told you." It's not a question. I refuse to confirm his suspicion and remain silent, I feel the other's gazes on me but ignore them as I focus on the two sitting opposite me. "Where is she?" I frown.

"What?" Saint and Crue share a look before turning back to me.

"We tried to find her at the hotel you said you booked, she was never there, Alexa. We tried to find her when we got back to campus but she had moved out of her dorm. We even tried to call but she blocked us." My eyes widen, what the fuck is Katie doing and why is she hiding? Before our conversation can continue an older gentleman interrupts us. I recognize him as the man from the penthouse, he's Corvin's lawyer.

"Sorry I'm late, boys," he says in a rush. He smiles at each of us girls. "Ladies." We all nod and say hello as he pulls up a chair and sits at the other end of the table between Darius and Beck, then pulls out a manila file. "Okay, I have everything drafted. I just need Miss Sutton to sign, then I'll be on my way to the police station." I steel my spine and gape at the guy.

"What?" I rasp out. Corvin places a hand on my thigh under the table drawing my attention back to him. The look in his brown eyes begs me to listen before I lose my shit.

"Troy, want to give us a minute?" he says without taking his eyes off me. I hear the man stand up and walk away. Corvin looks around the room making sure no one is within earshot and I begin to worry now as his face takes on a serious look. "You know Troy is our lawyer." I nod but still don't understand where he is going with this. "Us all being here at this restaurant is an alibi." My brows jump to my hairline. "We needed to be seen in public in case shit went south."

"What are you trying to say, Reaper?" I ask warily. He

looks around at the others before focusing back on me, he reaches out and cups my cheek.

"Troy is here because I need you to sign those papers."

"Why?" I ask with a bite to my tone.

"Because we are suing Jason and his family for child pornography." I gasp and recoil in my chair, his hand drops back to his lap and he quickly grips my hands in his to keep me in place. "Katie was able to track the original source of where the photos came from. You were sixteen and underage, Alexa. He sold those photos of you to…" He cuts his gaze to Saint. I follow his line of sight and guilt is written all over the jokester's face.

"My dad." My mouth drops open in shock. "My father owns a tech company. He thought he would be able to buy the pictures, sell them to the tabloids and threaten me with Corvin's career."

"Why the fuck would he do that and what do I have to do with any of this shit?" I ask.

Saint smiles sadly. Crue rests his hand on top of his shoulder in silent support. "Because he wants to teach me a lesson for taking down Darius's dad and being able to pay back every cent he ever gave me. He used you to get to Corvin, knowing that I would do anything for my best friend, even giving up my dream of being drafted and go back to him so I could take over the family business."

I'm so confused. "I don't get it," I say honestly.

"My father can't inherit my mother's trust fund unless I take over the company, it was a stipulation in the will. He has until I turn twenty-one to get me back or the money automatically goes to me."

"But, aren't you like rich?"

He nods but I can see there is more to this. "My mother came from a wealthy family. They own vineyards, and those wineries make more money in a month than my father does in a year. I promise I won't let him get away with what he has done to you."

"Rich people can never be happy unless they have everything," I mutter, pissed off that I was used and exposed to the world because of a grudge between father and son.

"If you sign those papers, Jason will pay for what he did to you and then some." The way his eyes darken tells me there is more to this.

"You're not just going to sue him, are you?" I see the war in his eyes, he doesn't know if he should lie or speak the truth so I push on. "You wouldn't need an alibi if I was just signing papers, you plan to go after him, don't you?"

A whoosh of air escapes him before his eyes harden. "I'm not going to let that piece of shit get away with what he's fucking done to you. He is going to suffer first, before I rip everything he holds near and dear away from him. By the time we're done with him, he won't have two fucking pennies to rub together."

I search his gaze trying to find any sign of him joking, but I can't find one. "He's a snitch, Corvin," I hiss.

A dark smile graces his handsome face. "Oh, I know, baby. Have faith, we got this." If his words were supposed to put me at ease, they don't. Maybe I'm a shitty person for being happy at the fact Jason will get a dose of his own medicine and know what it feels like to be at the mercy of someone else's fists and not be able to stop them. Corvin leans in, his lips brushing against the shell of my ear sending a shiver down my spine. "Be a good girl and sign the papers." The bastard sits back in his seat and shoots me a wink, knowing hearing those two words from him turns me the fuck on.

After signing the papers, Corvin instructs Troy to wait until morning to lodge them. A sick sense of satisfaction rolls through me knowing that he is about to get his soon. I feel kind of bad that his parents will be brought into this but they both knew about their son's addiction. His mother even saw the evidence of his abuse toward me and just turned a blind eye. It was easier for his parents to ignore their son's wrong-doings rather than cause a scandal, fucking rich people, man. Rather than doing the right thing they would ignore it and turn a blind eye so they don't make the front page of the news.

Once we finish eating, Darius slips the waiter a thick stack of bills before leading them out the back entrance. That's when it clicks, everyone saw us all enter but no one will see us leave so if Jason was to go to the cops, we would have over thirty witnesses that saw us here. We pile into the cars and head back to the penthouse. Instead of pulling into the garage where he normally parks the car he drives around the back of the building and parks in the staff car park. I look over at him and frown.

"No cameras around here or in the service elevators," he says in a matter-of-fact tone.

"Oh," I manage to say before following him out of the car and meeting the others at the back entrance where we take the service lift up to the penthouse. The tension in the air is thick. I look over at Beck's smile. His son is fast asleep in his hold and the sight of this burly guy who looks like he can crush skulls with his bare hands being so tender and soft toward his baby boy is a beautiful sight to see. Leah leans in closer to me and whispers.

"Becky's a DILF." Unable to stop it, laughter bursts out of me. I clamp my hand over my mouth so I don't wake Dawson.

"I fucking heard that shit, Goldie," Darius growls from Leah's other side.

"So, did I." Both of us look over at Val who is grinning. "And honestly, I one hundred fucking percent agree. My baby daddy is definitely a *dad I'd like to fuck*." Corvin and Darius groan, Beck on the other hand just shoots his girl a wink.

"I vote Beckett stays in Alaska and never comes back," Corvin grits out. Beck glares at his friend.

"The fuck did I do?" he whisper shouts just as the doors open.

"Be born," Corvin deadpans and stalks out of the lift. I race after him and manage to catch him by the arm just as he enters the living room. He spins around and glares down at me.

"Why are you mad?" I ask. I can see it in his eyes and I roll my lips over my teeth to keep from laughing. He's jealous.

"Swear to God, if you start saying half the shit my sister does about that asshole, I'm taking it out on your orgasms." Laughter breaks out from the others behind me, while I stand here gaping up at him.

"I just laughed at what she said!" I defend.

He throws his hands in the air frustrated. "Fucking hell, just stay away from Beckett," he snaps.

"Why the fuck am I always getting blamed?" I spin around to find Beck standing there looking pissed off. Dawson is no longer in his arms so I assume Val is putting him to bed in the spare room.

"They hate that you're so pretty, Becky," Leah sassily replies from her seat on Darius's lap. Darius grips his girl-friend's hips, lifts her off his lap and places her on the sofa beside him, then glares at her.

"After that comment, I hope you enjoy being on your knees for the next week, Goldie." Corvin groans, Leah looks like she is about to have a stroke and Beck still looks pissed off. I look to the other sofa to see Crue and Saint both sitting there with shit eating grins on their faces, that's when the tension between Darius, Beck and Leah makes sense. She slept with Beckett!

Turning back to Corvin, I smile up at him. He keeps his

face blank as he stares down at me. "I like your friends. They're cool and all that but believe me when I tell you, Reaper, none of them could handle my crazy ass. I don't plan on having a threesome, foursome or anysome with any of them." My words seem to put his jealous ass at ease and the tension in his shoulders eases as he reaches out and pulls me into him, hugging me tight as he places a kiss on the top of my head. Katie told me his ex, Lana, cheated on him and I know that his sister's playful banter with Beck worries him that I'll start doing the same, but I won't. I'd never do that shit to him because I don't see another guy but him.

Corvin is my gravity and I'd never do anything to jeopardize what we have, I love him way too fucking much for that to happen.

CHAPTER TWENTY-SEVEN

We pull up on the other side of the park in my Range Rover where I told the fucker to meet me. I brought an empty duffle with me for visual purposes only in case he's watching from a distance and spooks when he doesn't think I have the money. I look to Crue who is driving. Beck, Saint and Darius sit in the back.

"Circle back to the other side and come in from behind." Crue nods as I get out of the car and walk through the dark park. After five minutes, I feel eyes on me and stop near the outskirts of the trees that border around the park. I slowly turn around to see Jason standing there. The moon is our only source of light out here. He takes a couple steps closer and I take my time as I look him over. The guy looks fucking strung out, his eyes constantly darting from side to side and he's unable to stop rocking back and forth, he's coming down.

"Hand it over," he rushes out. I drop the bag on the ground beside my feet, making his eyes narrow. "Don't fuck me around. I got other pictures of her—"

"Did you feel like a man pushing her around? Or what about when you would see her cover the bruises you left on her with makeup?" I'm vibrating with rage, the need to feel his bones break beneath my fists thrums through me.

"She should have shut her fucking mouth, the stupid bitch —" I don't give him a chance to finish before I'm launching at him and landing a jab to his nose. I feel the bones break. He stumbles backward and nearly falls to his ass but Beck and Darius are there catching his arms and holding him up. He struggles in their hold as he looks around, when he sees Crue and Saint standing on either side of me, he pales. "What the fuck is this?" he shouts. I relish the sound of fear in his voice.

"This is your reckoning, you worthless sack of shit, I'm going to take everything from you like you did to her," I sneer. His eyes widen as I come at him again, this time I don't stop at one punch, I keep going. It's like a haze has come over me and I see nothing but the need to make him hurt like he did to my girl.

"Corvin, stop," Saint shouts as he and Crue wrestle me away from the sack of shit. I shake my head to clear it and gape at the sight in front of me. Jason hangs limply in Beck and Darius's hold with his chin against his chest, even without a light I can see the blood that is smeared all over his face. "Let's go, now."

Darius and Beck release him from their hold and he drops to the ground. I have to force myself to turn away from him and follow after the others or I know I'll end up killing him. I ride shotgun while Saint drives and the others climb in the back, we're all silent until we pull around the back of my building. Saint kills the engine and none of us make a move to get out. My adrenaline is still running high.

Saint looks over at me and whatever he sees on my face has him speaking to distract me from my thoughts. "The hostile takeover for my dad's company is next Monday. I want you all back at CHU with me." I stare at him in disbelief. We never pushed the issue with Devon, knowing this was hard for Saint, but hearing him say the words finally makes me so fucking proud of him. "Once I do this, we'll finally be free of all this shit and be able to finally… chill."

I haven't given much thought to what that would look like. With Devon gone, we wouldn't have to worry so much about him trying to fuck us from behind the scenes. Beck is due to move back in a couple of months, and Darius and Leah plan to move back to CHU in a couple of weeks. I need to get my ass back there and sort out shit with that house and see Cody.

"We'll be there," Beck answers for us. Now I just need to convince Alexa to try to take her last two exams online because I'm not leaving her behind.

"When do you head back to New England?" Crue asks.

"Two weeks," I answer dejectedly. I hate that I'm going to be away from my girl, she still has at least a couple of years left of school and I won't ask her to give up her dreams for mine.

"Would she transfer to CHU?" Darius asks. I mull over his words for a second.

"I never thought about it to be honest," I reply.

"Maybe ask her, because Leah will be there, at least that way she can stay with us and I'll keep an eye on her." Darius has a point.

"And make sure you keep your dick in your pants," Crue snarks. I turn and pin him with a glare, which causes the prick to laugh. We sit in the car for a long time, just talking shit and making plans for the future but the moment my phone vibrates in my pocket, all my focus is on the message from my girl.

JAIL BAIT

I miss you!

How much do you miss me?

JAIL BAIT

Enough to be fingering myself while texting you one handed.

"Fuck," I snap, then look to my boys and salute the fuckers. "I'm out, thanks and all that shit, got a girl to do so, later." The four of them all laugh at me as I bail on them. I've never, and I mean never, bailed on my boys for a girl before. They were my number one but now, I have a girl that I love, and the need to be with her always is fucking strong.

One week later

Sitting here staring out the windshield, I don't really see anything, I'm too lost in my own thoughts. So much has happened this past week. I managed to convince Alexa to transfer to CHU, it only took denying her to come a few times before she agreed. I had her dorm room packed up in record time and her transfer put in at WFU within a day. Her and me, with the help of Saint and Crue, cleaned out the old house and got it set up for D, Leah and my girl. It feels good having our home base back, this is the house we always come back to and I know that isn't going to change any time soon. The hostile takeover went better than we could have thought. Devon somehow got wind of what was happening and fled. Saint seems to think we haven't seen the last of his father and I'm inclined to agree with him. Devon isn't the type to cut and run and not retaliate.

"Do you want me to go with you?" I shake my head to clear it, look over at my girl and smile. I have one week left before I have to go back to New England, I'm going to miss her so fucking much.

"Nah, I got to do this alone, baby." She nods and leans

over the console placing a kiss on my lips, before she can pull away I grip the back of her head and deepen the kiss, moaning into her mouth. She shoves against my chest and I reluctantly let her go but scowl in her direction.

"We are not making out or fucking in the car when my sister is buried right over there." I cringe and smile sheepishly.

"My bad," I mutter before kissing her cheek and getting out of the car. I take a deep breath and force myself to walk toward Cody's grave. Being back here is fucking hard. This town used to feel like home, CHU was my playground. Me and the guys owned that place but now, none of this means anything to me. I found my real home and It's not a place, it's a person. They say home is where the heart is and my heart is with Alexa. I come to a stop in front of her tombstone, sadness washes over me at the sight of her name.

Kneeling down I reach out and place my hand atop the stone. I wish more than anything I could change the outcome of how her life ended. "Hey, gorgeous," I say quietly as I run my fingers along her name. "I know you're probably pissed at me for taking so long to come see you but… it's been hard. No, that's a lie… I-uh, ran away and chose not to deal with losing you. I was a coward and hid away from my problems. Well, I tried to hide as best I could until your crazy ass sister found me." I laugh fondly as I think back to how Alexa came into my life. I take a shuddering breath before continuing. "I'm so sorry I couldn't love you the way you wanted me to. You deserved so much more than me. I was an idiot and treated you wrong. I should have answered that call, I should have been there but I was too much of a dick. I promise you, Cody, I'll never do that to Alexa. On my life, you have my word that I'll always be there for her and show up any time she needs me. I won't make the same mistake twice." Leaning forward, I place a kiss on her stone and push to my feet. "I'll come back and see you soon, gorgeous."

Walking away I feel like a weight has been lifted off my chest, I now feel like I can finally let go of my past and focus on my future. Speaking of my future, I smile at the sight of my raven-haired beauty sitting on the bonnet of my Spyder— I had it shipped out here. She looks like a wet dream and fuck my cock twitches in my shorts at the thought of fucking her on the bonnet of my car.

"You're giving me fuck me eyes, Reaper," she says as I close the space between us and place my hands either side of her legs, then lean in, ghosting my lips over hers.

"I need to be balls deep inside you, jail bait." Her eyes become hooded at my words and her breathing grows shallow.

"Fuck me hard and make me come on your cock, then I might just tell you my secret." I almost miss the last part of what she said thanks to the mental images playing on a reel in my mind. I pull back, putting some space between us. Reaching up, I grip a handful of her hair and yank her head back, drawing a loud moan from her. Fuck, that sound has my cock rock hard.

"Tell me now or you'll be on your knees and I'll be the only one coming." The way her eyes darken tells me that her sucking my cock isn't a punishment and more of a reward. Fuck, she is perfect.

She holds my gaze as she reaches up and locks her arms around my neck, then draws me in closer so she is the one ghosting her lips over mine. "The new semester doesn't start till September." I frown not following what she's saying. She darts her tongue out and licks my lips, drawing a pained groan from me. "You're not going back to New England alone, Reaper, I'm coming with you." I reel back and stare down at her with wide eyes, a satisfied smile is plastered across her face.

"You're... coming with me?"

She nods excitedly. "Only for the summer, then I have to

come back here and start school—" I don't let her finish, I grab her waist and lift her into my arms. She locks her arms and legs around me. I smile up at her, feeling fucking grateful and happy as fuck that she'll be with me. "I'll come to you every holiday or whenever I can. I want this to work, Corvin, I can't lose you." The worried look in her eyes spares me.

"Baby, you and me are forever. I promise you, you will never lose me, Alexa. Every part of me is yours. Nothing in this world scares me except for the thought of losing you." She melts into me and places a tender kiss to my lips.

"I love you, Reaper."

"I love you too, jail bait. Now, get the fuck in the car so I can get your ass home and fuck it on the bonnet."

EPILOGUE

Alexa

Seven months later… December

Being back at the cabin with everyone feels amazing. Well, being able to spend Christmas with my fiancé—yes! You read that shit right. Corvin proposed to me Christmas morning in front of everyone. Best fucking Christmas present ever. I never expected to turn eighteen a couple weeks ago and then be engaged within the same month, but I'm not even mad about it. So much has changed in the past couple of months. Beck and Val got married over Thanksgiving break. It was an intimate wedding at the resort in Alaska. Corvin couldn't make it in person but he was there via Facetime. Beck, Val, and Dawson bought the house next to the one Darius, Leah and I share. It's freaking cool having them as neighbors, now we can have girl's night all the time. Darius and Beck have to travel for work a lot, but they are both never gone at the same time.

Saint and Crue both got drafted, but neither of them was exactly ecstatic that they didn't make the same team. Saint now plays for the Seattle Seahawks and Crue plays for the

New Orleans Saints. As soon as I heard who Crue played for, I laughed my ass off and said to Corvin, he finally gets to play on Saint's team. We cut our stay short at the cabin as Crue and Saint have a game against each other tonight in Tennessee. We flew in on Boxing Day, and while Crue and Saint have been training with their teams, the rest of us have been sightseeing and enjoying our time together before Corvin heads back to New England. Beck leaves for Japan on the same day, leaving the rest of us at CHU. This is the hard part—I hate saying goodbye to Corvin. It never gets easier but the moment I finish school, I plan to open a garage in New England so I can be with him every day.

Holy shit!

That was the most intense game of football I have watched. I mean watching Corv play is always amazing but to watch our friends play on opposing sides was freaking epic. Saint's team lost, but not by much. The best part of the game was when it was over. Watching Crue run and jump at Saint, smiling wide was a sight to see. Everyone can see there is something there between them, but I don't think they have ever explored it.

"Swear to God if they are fucking some chick in there while we freeze our asses off, I'm going to knock their teeth out," Darius grits out as he pulls Leah in closer to his chest to keep warm. Beck and Val left already to take Dawson back to the hotel so he could bathe and get ready to meet us for dinner. I snuggle into Corvin's side, trying to siphon some of his body heat.

"Here they come," Leah says. Sure enough, the dynamic duo saunters toward us, smiling from ear to ear. We congratulated each of them quickly before retreating to the car and blasting the heat. The guys talk about the game the whole way and it honestly makes me smile hearing the passion in each of their voices. Darius and Beck may not play anymore, but I know they both love the game just as much as these three.

We pull up outside the restaurant. Corvin hands the keys to the valet as we all make our way inside, for an all-you-can-eat rib joint it seems pretty upper-class. The maître d' smiles and prepares to walk us to our table, but Crue waves her off as we spot Beck and Val at the back. We follow Crue and Saint through the crowded restaurant. A woman pushes back from her table and stands only to collide with Saint as she attempts to step out. Crue manages to reach and catch her before she can fall to the ground.

"Shit are you—" Saint clamps his mouth closed the moment he looks at the woman. Crue drops his hold on the woman like she burnt him. I peer around Crue only to have the same reaction as Saint, it's like seeing a ghost. The other three push forward to get a look at what's going on. The moment Leah sees Katie, she gasps. Katie has changed, her hair is now brown and she even has a tattoo that covers her whole arm. The tension between the three of them is tangible, they all look so angry but beneath that anger, you can see the want that lingers in each of the guy's eyes.

"Saint, Crue, what up, dudes?" Some guy says as he comes to stand beside Katie. He extends his hand toward Saint but he and Crue are both entranced by the dark-haired beauty in front of them, who has yet to say a word. The guy looks from the duo to Katie and frowns, then he does something that shocks the fuck out us all. He wraps his arm around her waist and draws her into his side, making it known without words that Katie is with him. "Well, it was good to see you guys but we need to head out." The guy doesn't wait for a response, he drags Katie away and like the broken-hearted boys they are, they watch her walkway. The worst part is just before she disappears out the doors, she looks back. Saint attempts to go to her but Crue places a hand on his chest stopping him.

"Who the fuck was that guy?" Leah asks. Corv wraps an arm around my waist and pulls me flush against him, my back to his chest.

"That was Jackson Rathborne, wasn't it?" Corv asks. I frown not knowing that name.

"I fucking knew it was that prick!" Darius growls.

Leah throws her hands in the air. "Would someone tell me who we are talking about?" I hum my agreement, not knowing who that guy is and why he's with Katie pisses me off.

The broken look on Saint's face crushes me, but the look of utter devastation on Crue's breaks my heart. "Jackson Rathborne was my best friend, and he's the one who outed me to my parents," Crue whispers brokenly.

"Jackson isn't just his ex-best friend, he's also Crue's cousin and that cunt is the reason his parents disowned him," Saint spits out, but something still doesn't sit right with me.

"Does Katie know who he is?" I ask. Saint's jaw locks as a dark look overshadows his face. Crue just looks devastated and betrayed.

"She knows exactly who that cunt is, she was the one who helped us find the dirt on him in case we ever needed it," Saint snaps, then turns to Crue. He reaches out and grips the back of Crue's neck pulling him in close and leaning his forehead against Crue's. This moment feels so intimate almost like we are intruding on their private moment. "She broke our hearts months ago, now she thinks she can fuck with us by being with that dog. She won't get away with hurting us twice." Crue nods stiffly as Saint releases him and walks away.

"She wasn't the only one who broke my heart," Crue mutters brokenly, the devastation in his eyes robs me of air. Not only did Katie leaving break his heart, Saint also pulled away from Crue and left him alone. He lost both the people he loved in one night.

Thank you!

Dear Lord this one fucking broke me.
Corvin was a bad boy in Darius and Beckett's books but in this one, he was a ruined, broken man who needed a bad bitch to save him. Cue Alexa motherfucking Sutton. This girl was a dream to write and honestly, we have nicknamed her Karma and I think it fits.
I fucking hope you loved this book because honestly, I have to say this one is one of my favorites.
I know you hate me a wee bit for that ending but, Saint and Crue's book Blindside will be coming soon, preorder now from Amazon.
If you would be so kind as to leave a review on Amazon, Bookbub and/or Goodreads that would be amazing.

PARANORMAL ROMANCE

<u>The Dream Series</u>

<u>The Dream Trilogy</u>

A Beautiful Dream

A Twisted Fate

A Beautiful Nightmare

Redemption

Anarchy

<u>Brutal Savages</u>

Savage Lies

Brutal Truth

Savage Beast

Brutal Beauty

MAFIA ROMANCE

<u>Murdoch Mafia Series</u>

Played By The Bishop

Tormented By The King

Tortured By The Knight

Tempted By The Queen

Turned By The Pawn

Ruined By The Rook

<u>Fairytales With A Twist</u>

Condemned Beast

SPORTS ROMANCE

<u>Playing For Keeps</u>

<u>Duet</u>

Offside

Touchdown

End Game

Hail Mary

Blindside

RH SPORTS

Hate Us Like You Mean It

Acknowledgments

Marcus, what can I say aside from thank you for the dick inspo and trying out all these positions with me. I'm excited to write the next book since its MFM, you down to add an extra in the bedroom? Asking for a friend…

My Alpha girls, Clare, Sarah and Tash. Thank you ladies from the bottom of my cold fucking dead heart, these books wouldn't be what they are without all your help and feedback, thank you and I love you! I know this book had some of you in tears and the others wanting to riot but I fucking love how it turned out.

My Army: Alicia, Amber, Angel, Ash, Barb, Charlotte, Cyndi, Debbie, Jasmine, Jen, Kahanna, Katelyn, Lakshmi, Lora, Lyndsey, Sarmi and Tess. Thank you ladies so fucking much for being the best freaking team an author could ask for, I owe you all so much for the love and dedication you give me.

Natasha Joanne, my love, I adore and can't thank you enough for all you do but swear to God, I'm glad this book is over so you'll stop nagging me for more!

My editor, Lizz, fucking hell you are amazing! Thank you so much for continuing to love each of my books and making them all pretty for me. You truly are a star my friend.

My sprint partner, Jaye Pratt. Thank you for writing with me… most days when you weren't distracted on TikTok *eye roll*

My babies, I fucking love you both so much and I am so thankful that you chose me to be your mum.

Leah Maree, my love as per usual you smashed this fucking

cover out of the park. You are so beyond talented and I am in
awe of you.
Sarah Wilson, I have to give you a special shout out, babe,
because you helped me mold each of these characters and
they are what they are because of you, thank you my love.
Last but not least, you, my amazing readers, mean everything
to me! Without you none of this would be possible, thank you
for your continued support and reading my books, it still
stuns me to get messages from you telling me you love my
books. I really am living my dream and that's thanks to you.
Sam

xx

About the Author

Samantha Barrett is a dark romance, PNR author who loves to write out-of-the-box stories. She is originally from the land of the long white cloud, New Zealand. She is totally fluking her way through this whole author gig, if she isn't writing you can find her kicking back with her kids and husband with a bag of chips and a glass of wine in her hand.
Sam loves Twilight and is a TWIHARD proudly.